A
Harlequin
Romance

OTHER

Harlequin Romances

by MARJORIE LEWTY

Many of these titles are available at your local bookseller
or through the Harlequin Reader Service.

For a free catalogue listing all available Harlequin Romances,
send your name and address to:

HARLEQUIN READER SERVICE,
M.P.O. Box 707, Niagara Falls, N.Y. 14302
Canadian address: Stratford, Ontario, Canada.

or use order coupon at back of book.

ALL MADE
OF WISHES

by

MARJORIE LEWTY

HARLEQUIN BOOKS   TORONTO
WINNIPEG

Original hard cover edition published in 1974
by Mills & Boon Limited.

© Marjorie Lewty 1974

SBN 373-01819-3

Harlequin edition published October 1974

Printed in Canada

' It is to be all made of sighs and tears
All made of passion and all made of wishes.'
                    Shakespeare: *As You Like It*

CHAPTER I

AVERIL breathed a sigh of relief when the desolate emptiness of Bodmin Moor was behind her and the little blue Mini was buzzing cheerfully along towards the outskirts of the town.

If it hadn't been for Kevin, and his bland certainty that she would always act on his advice and do what *he* thought best, she wouldn't have come this way at all; she would have chosen the other, gentler road from Okehampton.

'You'd better go by the south road,' Kevin had instructed her before she left Exeter this morning. 'I wouldn't trust this boneshaker you've bought not to let you down at any moment, and the middle of Bodmin Moor wouldn't be the best spot to be stranded in, especially now, before the start of the summer season, when there won't be much traffic about.'

He had been quite right, of course. Kevin usually was right, which sometimes annoyed Averil, who often had an urgent need to do things *her* way, however risky, or even just plain foolish.

Kevin hadn't been at all enthusiastic about her buying the Mini in the first place. Last night she had driven straight from the garage to show it off to him, and parked proudly outside his art boutique, which was situated in a side road near the main Exeter shopping area.

Probably she had been hoping for too much when she had imagined he would be as thrilled with the little car as she was, but she certainly hadn't expected his blank disapproval. He didn't say it in so many words, but he obviously thought she was mad to rush off and buy a second-hand car almost the minute she had passed her test. What he said was, 'It would have been better to wait until I had time to look it over for you.'

'But I might have lost the chance altogether then,' Averil had wailed. 'There were three other people after her. The man at the garage said—'

'Averil, *dear*!' The crinkles in Kevin's forehead had risen to meet the crinkles in his fair hair. 'When will you learn something about business? The man at the garage said—' he mimicked tolerantly. 'Don't you know you never believe anything anyone says when they want to sell you something?'

But she had insisted firmly that she was sure the Mini was a bargain, and that it would serve her well for years, just as the garage man had promised. And she needed a car so badly, so that she could get down to see Sara more often. 'She sounded rather depressed last time she wrote. I'm so glad I'm going down today to cheer her up.'

'I'd have thought your sister would be too busy, just before the start of the holiday season, to get depressed,' Kevin said practically. 'Isn't the hotel doing well?'

Averil frowned rather worriedly. 'I don't really know. But I don't think it's anything to do with the Cormorant. It's more likely to be something— personal.'

Kevin hadn't been interested in Sara's personal problems and he had started to give Averil detailed instructions about her route, ignoring the fact, which he knew very well for she had often told him, that she had lived in Cornwall since she was ten, and knew all the routes from Exeter to St Cloe like the back of her hand. He had adjusted his important, heavy-framed glasses and said, 'I've put my own map in your car, and I've written out the route for you. You can have lunch at Tavistock; you should be there about lunch time. There's a place where you can get quite a decent meal. I've jotted down the name.'

Suddenly it hadn't been worth arguing about. 'Thank you, Kevin, you've been to a lot of trouble,' Averil said.

And so he had, she told herself now, and she was a horrid ungrateful little pig because she had found it absolutely necessary to travel by a different route from the one he had marked down, and to buy sausage rolls and a bottle of ginger beer to have in the car, instead of lunching in a civilised way at a restaurant.

Often Averil deplored this tendency to contrariness in herself. She would, she imagined, have preferred to be feminine and yielding like her elder sister Sara (although if Sara had been a little less feminine and yielding and hadn't run off and married that awful man, it would have saved a lot of heartache!) But Sara had been born soft and dark and gentle, whereas Averil was a tawny girl, with hair the colour of a ripe conker, and blue-grey eyes that could sparkle with fun or glint like icicles at a moment's notice. At twenty-two she was still learning to cope with her temperament. It wasn't easy.

It would have served her jolly well right, she berated herself now, if the Mini had let her down in the middle of Bodmin Moor. But it hadn't. Except for the fact that the petrol gauge seemed to be stuck at 'Empty' the little car had behaved very well indeed. Still, she must find out about the petrol at the first garage she came to. There was still quite a long way to go to St Cloe. Meanwhile, with the worst of the journey behind her, she could relax and enjoy the drive. Up on the moor, near Jamaica Inn, the mist had been quite thick, but now the sun was breaking through and

9

the birds were singing and it was April. The road, which would no doubt be full of holidaymakers in a couple of months, was almost empty, but she was careful to glance occasionally in the rear mirror now and again. Kevin had taught her to drive—except for a couple of lessons from a professional teacher just before her test—and he had been very keen on that point. 'Always keep an eye on traffic behind you as well as in front of you, and assume that all drivers are mentally deficient.'

She had admitted the wisdom of this advice, although she hadn't altogether liked his way of putting it. But Kevin had his Advanced Driving Certificate hanging up on the wall in the office behind his boutique, so he had to be allowed to be right, on this point at least.

Perhaps it was thinking of Kevin at that moment that made Averil do the unforgivable thing for a tyro driver. She took one hand off the wheel to wind down the window and let in some of the air and sunshine. Worse, she took her eye off the road to find the window handle, and in so doing she allowed the car to 'wander' to the offside. Not very much, not dangerously perhaps, but suddenly a horn screamed from behind and she held her breath for a moment of petrified terror as a sleek grey monster of a car swerved widely to pass, travelling at a speed which she felt sure was illegal.

In a flash the other car had passed, its horn blaring out again in what she assumed was a signal of rebuke. Then it was disappearing into the far distance, looking like a toy, with its shiny silver-grey paint glinting in the sunlight. Averil's heart was bumping about unpleasantly. She had not even caught a glimpse of the driver of the grey car, but he was certainly a reckless show-off to overtake at a speed like that. She decided piously that she must, after all, remember Kevin's advice to regard all other road users as mentally deficient. Breathing slowly and evenly to recover her composure, she drove on in a circumspect fashion towards Bodmin.

Soon the advertisements of a petrol station came into view. She slowed down carefully and signalled before turning in. Then she drew up at the correct distance from a pump and waited. She wished she knew how much petrol there was in the tank. The man at the garage last night had said there was ' about four gallons in her,' and when she said she was driving into Cornwall today he had quipped, ' Take you to Land's End and back.' But the petrol gauge needle, which had been flickering around the three-quarter mark when she started out, was now unmovingly pointing to ' empty.' She would have to ask the petrol pump attendant when he came.

But nobody came. There was a small building at the rear with a glass window through which she could see a woman with piled-up golden hair. One or two other cars were standing in the forecourt, and one car was stationed beside one of the other pumps, without its driver. It had an unpleasantly familiar look about it. She couldn't be sure, of course, because that unnerving moment had passed so quickly and unexpectedly, but the car at the other pump was long and sleek and silver grey. And somehow, she told herself pettishly, still smarting from that last accusing blare on the horn, it *looked* like the car that a mentally deficient road-hog might drive.

A man was approaching from the building at the rear. Ah, at last here was someone to attend to her! Then she looked again and saw that this was no garage man. He was walking towards the grey car, and her first thought was that they fitted each other very well. He was tallish and dark and he moved with an air of assurance, the kind of sublime confidence that goes with being a man and having money and position. Oh yes, it was certainly the road-hog in person, Averil decided, disliking him upon sight.

He strolled towards the grey car, stuffing some pound notes carelessly into a wallet. He opened the door and bent to get in, and then he seemed to notice her, sitting in the Mini. He paused, looking hard at her. Goodness, surely he wasn't going to have the nerve to lecture her on her driving?

He slammed his car door again and came over to her, leaning down to the Mini's open window. 'Are you waiting for petrol?' His voice was deep and lazy, the kind of voice you would expect from a man like that. Public school. Oxbridge.

'I was,' Averil replied coolly.

A smile flickered. His eyes, she noticed, were a very intense dark blue, the kind of eyes that are usually attributed to sailors, and his face was deeply tanned. Winter sports, no doubt. You could just imagine him swooping down the frozen slopes, or the Cresta Run, or whatever it was they swooped down, she thought hazily. His steady gaze was doing something very disturbing to her pulse, which she resented. Averil was quite accustomed to having men look at her, but this one was somehow different.

'You'll have a long wait, I'm afraid,' he said. 'It's all self-service here. Didn't you see the notice?'

She looked around—and saw it. 'No, I hadn't,' she said, with what she hoped was dignity. He *would* make a fool of her, of course, after nearly running her off the road. Yet another dominant male, being patronizing to a woman driver!

She glanced in alarm at the list of instructions at the side of the pump and was quite sure she would never be able to work the thing. She had often been with Kevin when he served himself with petrol, but hadn't been in any way involved in the proceedings. Kevin always liked to take charge of matters like that; he considered it in keeping with his masculine role. She wished the dark man would get into his beastly great car and go away and leave her to struggle.

But he showed no immediate intention of going away. He stood there looking at her as if he were enjoying it, which he probably was, for Averil, what with the heady excitement of driving her own car, together with the mixture of annoyance and agitation that his presence was arousing in her, was decidedly worth looking at. Her smooth cheeks were flushed and her eyes sparkled like hoar frost and her russet hair swung engagingly into her neck as she threw back her head to meet his gaze.

'Are you familiar with these gadgets?' He indicated the petrol pump. 'Or shall I show you how to work it?'

For a moment she was torn between the desire to demonstrate her independence and her alarm at the very idea of trying to cope alone. Common sense triumphed. 'Thank you,' she said rather ungraciously, and then, conscience pricking, she added, 'If you have time.'

'Too much,' he said, in such a curious tone of voice that she knew he was really making the comment to himself and not to her at all.

He opened the door of the Mini for her to get out. Standing by his side she saw that he was even taller than she had thought. She was by no means a small girl herself, but her head barely reached to his shoulder.

He pointed to the chart of instructions. 'It's really quite simple. First, press this red button. That's to alert the glamorous lady in the cash office back there. Second, select the grade of petrol you need.' He glanced at the Mini, but not, she noticed, disparagingly as Kevin had done when he first saw it. 'Two star— three star?'

'I don't know,' she admitted, wishing she had asked the man at the garage. Then, because that sounded too feeble for words, she explained, 'I only bought the car yesterday.'

'I see. You've just begun to drive.' It was a statement, not a question. 'Well, let's try two star and you can change over at the next fill if you think it's necessary. Now then, unscrew cap on petrol tank, pull out hose, press bar underneath, and hey presto, all you have to do is to keep your eye on the indicator dial and stop when you reach the desired amount. Here, you try it yourself.'

He handed her the hose and she pushed it inside the open pipe on the car and pressed gingerly. Petrol spurted under pressure, the end of the hose seemed to pulse with a life of its own, jumping out of her hand so that the back of the car was deluged with the pungently smelling liquid.

Averil leapt backwards with a squeal. 'Oh dear, that wasn't clever at all.'

'We all have to begin some time,' he said. 'Try again and let me help you.' She picked up the hose and his hand covered hers, firm and strong. His fingers pressed hers against the trigger of the hose. It was quite ridiculous how her heart began to thump —ridiculous and humiliating. She tried to concentrate on what was happening, but almost immediately, it seemed, the tank overflowed with another splurge of petrol.

He hooked back the hose and eyed her with amusement. 'It's a micro tank you've got there, not a mini. Either that or you didn't really need petrol at all.'

'I suppose I didn't. I just thought I might.' She explained about the petrol gauge and he put his head inside the car, switched on the ignition and peered at the dial. 'Probably an electrical fault. I'd have it seen to if I were you,' he said, straightening up again. 'Otherwise you may be continually dry-cleaning your clothes without really intending to.'

'Oh!' She stared at him guiltily. 'Did you get splashed?' He was wearing a burgundy red jacket and pale fawn trousers and his whole outfit looked very new and very expensive. To her horror she saw a large, spreading damp patch on the right trouser leg. 'Oh, I'm terribly sorry!'

He glanced down carelessly. 'Did I catch it too? I was thinking of your coat.'

There was an identical patch near the hem of her swingy green coat. 'That doesn't matter; but I do really feel awful about your trousers. It will probably leave a horrid ring-mark when it dries.' For no reason she suddenly remembered how annoyed Kevin had been last week when she was helping him to polish some silver candlesticks he had bought for his boutique, and she had spilled some of the cleaning fluid on his sleeve. He hadn't lost his temper, of course, Kevin never lost his temper. He had pretended to make a joke of it, saying that for a girl who relied on her deftness of touch to make and repair jewellery she could be extremely ham-handed on occasion.

But this man didn't seem annoyed, nor did he make

a joke of it. He said, 'Please don't look so worried. It really is of no importance.'

He probably had several pairs of elegant trousers stowed away in an elegant travelling case in the boot of his elegant car. Still, it was nice of him to take it so well. She smiled at him uncertainly, her first opinion of him becoming somewhat blurred. 'Well, thank you for your help,' she said. 'Where do I pay for the petrol I've wasted?'

He was still there when she came out of the cash office, and as she drove carefully away he raised a hand in salute, leaning against the bonnet of the grey car as if he had all the time in the world to kill, which seemed odd when she remembered the mad speed he had been driving at recently.

Between Bodmin and St Austell Averil found herself glancing in her driving mirror even more frequently than was strictly necessary, and when no silver grey car loomed up out of the distance and swished past her, she began to think that he must have taken the road to the north coast. Perhaps he was going to Padstow for the famous 'Obby Oss' Festival on the first of May. That attracted many visitors and sightseers, although he didn't look quite the type to enthuse over an ancient folklore festival.

Just as she had almost given up the idea that she might see it again, the grey car came up from behind, drew level and passed her with a friendly hoot, travelling at a more circumspect speed than before. She caught a glimpse of a dark head and suntanned face, and saw a hand raised in brief salute as he passed.

Ahead, the road was under repair, with temporary traffic lights. The lights turned to red just as she reached them. She pulled up and waited, watching the grey car growing smaller and smaller as it streaked into the distance and finally disappeared round a bend. The lights changed to green and she let in the clutch with a little sigh. Forget it, chum, she instructed herself, and don't be such an idiot. You'll never see the man again.

As she turned off the main road into the narrower road that twisted and turned and eventually came out at St Cloe, that last thought seemed quite unreasonably sad.

The Cormorant, the small residential hotel which Averil's elder sister managed, was situated in a wooded valley below the village of St Cloe. Their father had taken over the hotel when he retired from the Navy twelve years ago. Sara had been seventeen then, and Averil nearly eleven. To Averil the change from living in Portsmouth had been like being transported to fairyland. She had been happy to spend her school holidays in the tiny sandy cove below the hotel, reached by a path that wound down between high banks and ended in a shallow flight of steps cut out of the rock. Here she had spent her school holidays, reading, swimming, collecting pebbles and shells, sometimes sailing when her father had time to take her.

She was alone a great deal of the holidays, for her mother had died many years ago, and Sara, at seventeen, was turning into a dark-eyed beauty who had all the young men visitors competing for her company. It was to Eliot Dunn, a naturalist and writer who owned a small cottage nearby, that Sara turned most often, and for a time it seemed as if she was really serious about him. Then suddenly, when she was eighteen, Sara fell wildly in love with a man from London, a journalist who was spending a few weeks here covering the making of a TV film.

Within a month they were married. Within a year

Sara was back at the Cormorant, with a baby a few weeks old, her marriage in ruins. And at the Cormorant she had stayed ever since, helping their father in all departments of the hotel, so that she could stand in anywhere at a moment's notice, learning the job the hard way from the bottom up. Three years ago an old war injury had begun to undermine the Commander's health, and Sara had gradually taken over the management. When a few months later their father died, she had quietly slipped into his place. The hotel's owner, Robert Frewins, an old friend of the Commander, had been happy with the arrangement, and Sara had made a success of it. The Cormorant catered for people who liked a very quiet holiday in a spot well off the beaten tourist track. Visitors returned year after year to enjoy the peace and beauty and the excellent food and comfort provided. Sara had seemed content and almost happy and her boy, Adrian, had grown up into a tough, lovable young rascal who had recently started as a boarder at a school in Truro.

Then, a few weeks ago, Averil had noticed a change in the tone of her sister's letters. Nothing definite, just a kind of uneasiness. Perhaps she was missing Adrian. Or perhaps she was giving way once more to the fits of depression that had attacked her at intervals for several years after the breakdown of her marriage. Whatever it was, Averil had decided to close up temporarily the tiny studio in Exeter where she was managing to make a small reputation for her handmade jewellery, and go to St Cloe to see for herself.

And now she was nearly there. She turned off the coast road into a road still narrower, which brought her finally to the village of St Cloe, with its colour-washed cottages and old spired church. It had rained a little in the night and everywhere looked fresh and trim, ready for the beginning of summer. The little gardens were ablaze with the last of the wallflowers and forget-me-nots, the hanging sign outside the Ship Inn swung gaily in the breeze, and in the forecourt of the garage her old friend Tom Berry was polishing a customer's car.

The temptation to stop and show off the Mini to Tom was too much for her. She drove up with a flourish, waved through the window and called out, 'Hullo, Tom, look what I've got!'

Tom stopped polishing and ambled across to her. He was tall and stringy, the face under his thatch of grey hair weathered to a fine mahogany shade. In his young days he had been a fisherman, looking after his father's three fishing boats in Mevagissey, but when the fishing seemed on the decline he had bought this little garage and pottered about here happily ever since.

He was pleased to see Averil and satisfyingly impressed with the Mini. 'Nice little job, arn' 'ee?' he purred, stroking the polished blue bonnet. 'We'll be seein' more of 'ee, then, Miss Av'ril? Your sister'll be glaad, I reckon, down there—' with an inclination of his head in the general direction of the Cormorant, below the village.

Averil smiled at him. 'Yes, I'm hoping to come down much more often this summer. It's ages since I was here, in fact I haven't seen my sister since Christmas. Have you seen her around lately, Tom? How do you think she is?'

Tom took off his faded Army beret and rubbed his forehead. 'Ah, well, I reckon she'll be a mite bothered about this—what do they call it?—take-over, arn' it? Rob Ellis from the Ship was tellin' me the other day. He knows 'bout it, being in the hotel line hisself, so to speak.'

'Take-over, Tom? Takeover of what?'

'Of the Cormorant, I s'pose, but you'd best aask Rob. He'll tell you all 'bout it.'

'Thanks, Tom, I'll go and see if I can find him.' If there were anything worrying Sara about the hotel it might be better to have at least an inkling of what it was all about before she arrived.

At half past four the Ship's front door was locked, but Averil found Rob's wife in the little patch of garden round the back, hanging up some tea towels. Mrs Ellis was delighted to see her. Averil was a great favourite with the village folk, who had watched her grow from a leggy schoolgirl into the remarkably pretty girl she was now. She, in her turn, was fond of them all, and grateful to them for accepting her family, and not treating them as 'foreigners', as sometimes happened in Cornwall.

'Rob's out just now,' Mrs Ellis said. 'But come in and have a cup of tea, m'dear. It's brewing in the pot at this very moment. The children are with their dad and I thought I'd have a nice peaceful cuppa.'

Over a cup of tea and a slice of Mrs Ellis's saffron cake, Averil heard news of the family, and then asked the question which was troubling her.

'I've just been talking to Tom at the garage, and he said something about the Cormorant being taken over. Do you know anything about it, Mrs Ellis? I thought I'd like to know what it was about, before I go down there. I've had an idea that Sara has been worried lately, but I haven't seen her for some time, and she hasn't mentioned it in her letters.'

Mrs Ellis nodded sagely. 'Aye, I'd be surprised if she weren't worried. The rumour's been going around that old Mr Frewins has sold out to a big London company. What do they call it now? Some bird or other. Blackbird? Crow?' She rubbed her nose. 'Raven. Yes, that's it, Raven.'

'Raven Hotels? You mean that Raven Hotels have bought the Cormorant?' No wonder Sara's letters had sounded different lately, if that was true!

'That's the story that I've been told. But don't take my word for it. It's only what Rob's heard, and he's a great one for gossip is my Rob.' She beamed complacently. 'Hadn't you heard 'bout it at all?'

'Not a word. I must get along now, and find out what it's all about.'

'Aye, you'll be wanting to see your sister. Be stayin' long, will 'ee?'

'I don't quite know, Mrs Ellis. It all depends.' It all depended on what sort of a state Sara was in. A change of owners might be a real upheaval—especially as old Mr Frewins had left the running of the hotel in Sara's hands entirely.

She thanked Mrs Ellis for the tea and set the Mini's nose towards the sea and the Cormorant. Five minutes in second gear down the steep twisting hill brought her to the place where the lane ended in a grassy patch, with a gravelled space on the right which served as a car park for the few vehicles that found their way down here. Straight ahead, through the trees, Averil caught a glimpse of the sea, blue as blue on this April day, flecked here and there with white. She stopped the Mini and drew in a deep breath of salty air. It was all so dear and familiar; somehow even more dear now that she only came back occasionally. If Ravens had really bought the hotel perhaps soon she wouldn't be coming back at all.

She pushed that dark thought away and turned into the short, neat drive of the hotel.

The Cormorant had once been a private residence, built at the turn of the century by a Bristol merchant who wanted a retreat where—even in those comparatively leisurely days—he could get away from it all. After the first war, when it was extended and turned into a hotel, the local stone had been used, and the general effect now was of a pleasant, mellow building, smothered up to the first floor windows in exotic climbing plants that thrived in this sheltered climate. There were even a couple of palm trees in the garden, and just now the borders were bright with tulips and hyacinths. It all looked very well kept and thriving, thought Averil, as she parked the car and got out. Surely even Raven Hotels wouldn't want to change it?

The hall was empty and she went straight through to the office, tapped on the door and walked in. She had an immediate impression of Sara sitting at the desk, surrounded as usual by account books, letters, papers, all the clutter of a busy office, before her sister gave a little gasp of surprise and jumped up to hug her warmly.

'Averil darling, how lovely! I didn't expect you yet. How come? Did you get a lift? I thought you'd ring from the station when you got in, as you usually do.'

'Aha! I have a surprise for you.' Averil shifted some more books and sat down on the window seat.

'Not—you haven't brought Kevin with you?'

Averil grinned. 'Not this time, Sal. Sorry to disappoint you.' She was sometimes surprised that Sara, after the disaster of her own marriage, should seem so anxious to see her settled down. Perhaps it was because Kevin was so obviously serious-minded and dependable, and Sara's ex-husband had been quite the reverse. On the one occasion that Sara had met Kevin she had seemed most impressed.

But Averil hadn't come away to talk about Kevin. 'How are you, Sal? And how's Adrian? Is he liking his new school?'

'Loving it, thank goodness. He's made a splendid start there.'

'That's grand. And what about you?'

'I'm fine too. Everything's fine.'

'Is it?' Averil said with frank disbelief. 'Is it really? How about this sell-out to Ravens?'

Sara's dark head jerked up. 'You know about that? How—'

'It's common news up in the village. Why didn't you tell me what was brewing, Sal? I thought your letters sounded a bit off, lately. I've been trying to think what could be wrong.'

Her sister looked rueful. 'I might have known I couldn't hide anything when you were about. I never could, could I?'

'I hope not,' Averil said. 'I don't go much for secrets—not between us, anyway. Come on, tell. What's the position exactly? Is it really true that Ravens have bought the Cormorant?'

'I'm afraid it is,' Sara said in a voice of doom. 'Completion was last Friday. Uncle Robert Frewins came here to see me, straight from signing the deed at the solicitors'. He was rather cut up—he's been so interested in the place for so many years.'

'Why did he sell out, then?'

'Well, he's getting on now, and Aunt Lucy is younger than he is, and I think he feels he must get his capital into a more easily available state. So that it would be easier for her if he went suddenly. It wasn't a shock about selling the Cormorant; he told me ages ago that he might consider it. He's been awfully sweet—he even put in a good word for me with old Matthew Raven. But I doubt if that will carry much weight.'

Averil stared at her sister's clouded face. ' You don't mean that they won't keep you on?' she asked bluntly, and when she saw that Sara did mean just that, ' You *must* be mistaken, Sal. You run the place marvellously. They'd be crazy to make a change.'

Sara smiled gratefully at her young sister. ' Thanks, love, you're always a tonic. But this time I'm afraid it would take more than a tonic to convince me I'm mistaken. How much do you know about the Raven group?'

' Nothing, really, only the name.'

Sara nodded. ' No—well, I've been finding out about them lately. There's a little place called The Begging Dog on the edge of Dartmoor, Tavistock way. Ravens took it over about two years ago. I went there last week to have a look round and the manager gave me all the gen.' She met her sister's eyes levelly. ' Truly, Averil, I doubt if I shall make the grade.'

' They'll never get anyone to manage the Cormorant better than you do. What's so special about Ravens anyway?'

' Just about everything, I'd say. The company is owned by Matthew Raven. He's an elderly man who made his pile between the wars building houses, then he got bored with that and started collecting hotels.'

' *Collecting* hotels?'

' That's what it amounts to. He owns this chain of smallish super-luxury hotels dotted about the country, all in out-of-the-way spots which have some special appeal. The Dartmoor place, for example, has trout fishing and the moor to ride and walk in. They all have something to offer—golf, shooting, mountain climbing, every kind of recreation you can think of. They attract V.I.P.s for week-ends and short stays when it's hardly worth while going abroad. And for longer stays, when they're just after a real rest with everything laid on and no effort to make.'

Averil said sturdily, ' But you can cope with top people, Sal. How about that Mr Beaufort—he comes back year after year, doesn't he? And the barrister and his wife who wrote you such a glowing letter of appreciation.'

' Well, yes, I suppose I can, in a way. But the Raven set-up is different altogether. At the Begging Dog they have an Italian chef and a staff of waiters and stewards, all imported, I gather. I don't suppose the food is any better than Mrs Bulteel turns out, and probably the service isn't really as good. I've got two excellent girls from the village and another two part-timers just now. But you see what I mean, don't you? I get the feeling that Matthew Raven—they call him " The Old Bird ", by the way,—will want to put in one of his top flyers as manager here before long— someone like the man at the Begging Dog. He's a *very* smooth customer indeed.'

' You haven't heard anything definite though?'

' Not directly. Just a letter from London, informing me officially of the change in ownership and saying that I would be kept in touch with plans.'

' Indirectly, then?' Averil was sure that something special had happened to make Sara look so worried, and she meant to know what it was.

Sara sat silent, twisting her pen between her fingers. Finally she said, ' Would you say I have a suspicious nature, Averil?' and as her sister burst into a guffaw of laughter, ' All right then, I haven't. But I've got a horrid feeling at this very moment that I'm about to be *watched*.'

'Darling! You're imagining things. Sounds like an Agatha Christie story. You're letting this change-over get you down.'

'No, I'm quite serious. It only happened a short time before you got here. There was this Mr William Randall who'd booked in a few days back. Well, he turned up a short time ago and '—Sara's voice lowered dramatically—' he brought a letter from the Old Bird himself! Oh, it was civil enough; said he had hoped to visit us himself before this, but pressure of work, etc., etc. He would probably be making some altera-tions when the coming season was over. Meanwhile, just carry on as usual. And he was sending down this Mr Randall, who had just joined his staff and wished to become acquainted with the hotels, and would I give him every facility—and so on, and so on—'

Averil digested this information and then said reasonably, ' That doesn't sound as if you were going to be out on the mat tomorrow.'

' Not tomorrow, perhaps. I don't suppose the axe will fall until the end of the season.' Sara's soft mouth quivered suddenly. ' Oh, Averil, I'll never find another job like this. I've loved this place ever since I used to help Father when we first came here, years and years ago, and I've been here ever since, except for that time —you know. And Adrian loves it too, and he's settling down at school, and if I lost my job I shouldn't be able to afford to keep him on there, and—oh, it's all so wretched!'

Averil saw that she would have to take this thing seriously. ' What's he like, this Mr William Randall?'

' Exactly what you'd expect. Very pleased with him-self and obviously out of the top drawer. His car takes up half the space in the garage and he's at this moment prowling round the place, no doubt writing down everything in his little black book. I offered to show him round, but oh no, his High and Mightiness said he'd rather drift about on his own. Beastly snooper!' Sara sniffed.

Averil's eye had caught something moving outside the office window and she turned her head, and suddenly something very odd seemed to be happening in the region of her knees. In fact, it was lucky that she was already sitting down at the time. For, crossing the lawn from the back of the hotel in the direction of the small annexe, was a tall dark man, moving with an easy, nonchalant swing that was somehow familiar to her. He was wearing a dark red corduroy jacket and pale fawn trousers, and even from this distance she could see the ring left by a dried petrol stain.

She said in a choky voice, 'Sara—that's not him, is it? That isn't the man you've just been talking about?'

Her sister followed her look. 'That's the brute,' she said grimly. Then, looking back at her sister, 'Averil, what's up? You look as if—Averil, for pity's sake don't tell me you actually *know* the wretched man. He isn't a friend of yours, is he? That would be the last, the very last straw!'

Averil's eyes were still on the burgundy red back, disappearing through the annexe door. 'Heavens, no, he's not a friend of mine. I've only sort of—encountered him casually. I don't know him at all.'

But she had an odd, very strong feeling that—absurd though it might appear—she was going to know him very much better. And that, for some reason she couldn't quite define, she wasn't at all sure she wanted to.

CHAPTER II

Sara turned wide eyes on her sister. 'Where on earth did you meet him, Averil? I shouldn't have thought he was the kind of—' She broke off, flushing. 'I'm sorry, it's no business of mine, really.'

'Of course it is.' Once, years ago, the sisters had shared confidences easily, but since the divorce Sara had been withdrawn, sometimes touchy about personal things. Averil wished with all her heart they could get back to the old sisterly intimacy. 'Of *course* it's your business. We're buddies, remember? I sort of met him at a garage, on the way down here. Look, come outside and see what I've got to show you, then I'll tell all.'

Out in the forecourt she waved a triumphant hand towards the blue Mini, standing in lonely dignity on the sweep of gravel. 'My very own,' she announced with pride.

'*No*—really?' For a moment the anxiety disappeared from Sara's face, and she was the old Sara that Averil remembered from the time before her disastrous marriage: eager, vivacious, brown eyes sparkling, soft mouth curved into a smile. She had to hear about the car: how Averil had found it, where she had bought it, how old it was. She had to sit inside and admire the condition of the upholstery, the radio, everything.

Averil climbed in beside her. 'I'm afraid paying for her has taken the last of the money Father left me. Fitting up the studio cost quite a bit.'

Sara pulled a rueful face. 'Mine all went ages ago. That time Adrian was so ill—and the sanatorium in Switzerland—and fitting him out for school last autumn cost the earth.'

Averil nodded sympathetically. 'Everything's so frantically expensive. Still, I think the Mini's an investment, because it means that I can pop down and keep an eye on you much more often.'

'That will be lovely.' Sara sighed and added, 'If I'm still here, that is.'

'Now then, no more negative thinking.' Averil patted her sister's knee firmly. 'You'll have to get the old charm working and get Mr William Randall on your side.'

Sara wrinkled her nose. 'Not a hope, I can't bear his type. But you haven't told me where you met him.'

Averil launched into a lighthearted description of her encounter at the garage. 'And I ended up by drenching his exquisite cavalry twills with petrol.' She giggled. 'It was a good thing it was me and not you. He certainly won't be very impressed with *my* efficiency.'

Sara allowed herself a small, disdainful smile. 'He must have been livid.'

'Oh, I don't know. He didn't seem to mind particularly, but perhaps that was because one pair of trousers more or less didn't matter to him. He looked rather—' she closed her eyes, trying to remember '—rather frustrated. Like Adrian if you told him he couldn't go fishing when he wanted to, and he was wondering how to fill in the time. Perhaps he didn't really want to come down here at all, Sal?' Averil warmed to this possibility. 'Perhaps he's fed up with the whole assignment and he'll soon go away and turn in a good account of the Cormorant, and then you can go on just the same as before.'

'It's a nice thought,' said Sara sceptically. She wriggled out of the driving seat. 'But don't let's think about *him*, let's think about something nice. It's so lovely having you here, Averil.' She came round the car and gave her young sister an affectionate hug. 'Let's make the most of it. But I'm afraid I won't be able to get away from the grindstone much. I mustn't give this Randall beast the faintest excuse for accusing me of neglecting the job.'

Averil grinned. 'I thought we weren't going to talk about him.'

'He gets under your skin,' Sara admitted.

'Well, he won't get under mine. And don't worry about going out. I'll be quite happy just pottering around here.' Averil pulled her suitcase from the back seat of the Mini. 'How's business just now?'

'Quiet until the spring holiday at the end of May; after that we're pretty well booked up. I've only got three in at the moment. There's Miss Stevens who's been here all winter. She's a retired headmistress and quite a dear, really, though she looks a bit intimidating. And Colonel Bartram and his wife; he's regular Army and he was hit in the chest by a sniper when his regiment was in Northern Ireland, and eventually he was invalided out. He's a nice man—rather silent, but his wife makes up for that.'

They reached the front door and Sara said, 'I'll come up with you, then I must lend a hand in the kitchen until Lily arrives.' She led the way up the wide staircase on the right of the hall, and along a passage at the top. 'You could easily have had one of the guest rooms, Averil, but when I knew this man was coming I thought it might be wiser to put you in with me. It wouldn't do to let him think the manager's sister was occupying one of the best bedrooms.' She heaved a deep sigh. ' Oh dear, why did this have to happen? It was so easy with Uncle Robert Frewins. He would have been delighted for you to be as comfy as possible. But with these new people— I just don't know, and I feel I've got to watch my step all the time. You don't mind sharing?'

' Of course I don't, it'll be like old times,' Averil said cheerfully. ' Remember, we always doubled up in the high season, didn't we?'

Sara pushed open the door of a pleasant bedroom at the back of the hotel, overlooking the garages and the kitchen garden, and the green, hilly country beyond.

' I've put up a bed for you. You'll be all right here?'

' Fine.' Averil plumped down her case on the folding bed. ' Don't you bother with me, Sal, if you want to get on downstairs. Anything I can do to help?'

' No, thanks, love. Lily will be here soon. She comes in to wait at table in the evening. Everything's under control. Yes, I'd better go.'

But she didn't go. She stood at the window, her back to Averil. Then suddenly she swung round and said in a funny tight voice, ' I think you'd better know —Eliot's back in the cottage.'

Averil had to think quickly. What had happened between her sister and Eliot Dunn, all those years ago when Sara married so precipitately, she had never known. But when Sara went Eliot went too, and even after Sara returned Eliot's little summer cottage had remained empty.

' Is he really? He didn't sell the cottage, then, after all?'

' Evidently not.' Sara's apparent lack of interest did not deceive the other girl for one moment.

' Have you seen him? How does he look? Is he married?'

' I met him for a moment last week in the village.'
Sara flicked an imaginary spot of dust from the dressing table. ' He looks much the same. I wouldn't
know if he's married—there wasn't any wife in
evidence. Now I must go and give Mrs Bulteel a hand.
Dinner at the usual time, Averil.'

When she had gone Averil unpacked her case
thoughtfully. It was wonderful news that Eliot had
returned. In the family's early days here, when she
had been a schoolgirl and Eliot a well-known naturalist
with several books to his credit, she had hero-
worshipped him fervently. She had woven romantic
dreams about him and Sara, and imagined herself
boasting to the girls at school about her famous
brother-in-law. When Sara wasn't available he had
sometimes taken Averil with him on one of his trips
round the coast. She had sat happily in the small boat,
with its ancient outboard motor chugging away at the
back while he talked to her about the sea birds and
the strange creatures who lived in the pools and round
the entrances to the caves. She had crouched patiently
beside him in a hide among the rocks, while he waited
his chance to get a photograph of some domestic details
of a bird's life. One of his books, autographed ' To my
good friend Averil North ', still had pride of place in
the bookcase in her studio.

Yes, it would be marvellous to see Eliot again. Even
more marvellous if he were still unattached and if he
and Sara could get back on the old terms. Tomorrow,
she decided, would go to the cottage and try to find
him. Her spirits, which had been a trifle dampened
by Sara's mood, began to rise again.

She glanced at her watch. There was time to go
down to the sea before she changed into a dress for
dinner. She took off her coat, wrinkling her nose at its

faint smell of petrol, and pulled a thick Aran sweater over her slacks. She tied a bright green scarf round her hair, and after a quick glance in the mirror, ran down the back stairs and out of the side door. She wondered what point Mr William Randall had arrived at in his tour of inspection, and she was acutely aware that her heart was thumping nervously at the idea of seeing him again, possibly even getting to know him better. Sara might consider him an insufferable character, but she, Averil, preferred to make up her own mind about people.

As she reached the side door and crossed the short path leading to the back entrance of the hotel, a quick glance round showed her that he was nowhere in sight, and she felt relieved and disappointed at the same time. Out in the lane she slowed down and took herself to task; she didn't usually get the jitters like this about meeting new people. Why, the man probably wouldn't even recognise her as the girl he had casually helped at a petrol station. She didn't see any particular reason why she should register with him. He, on the other hand, was a man who couldn't fail to register vividly with any woman at all. He was primed with that dangerous and elusive quality known as masculine magnetism, she thought with a grin. Some men had it, others didn't. Its effect was immediate and uncomfortably strong—you were either repelled or attracted. Sara had been repelled, whereas she—*hadn't* been repelled.

She walked briskly along the lane towards the sea, sniffing with pleasure the spring scent of growing things. Her first visit, as always, must be to Methuselah. There he was, looking the same as ever, in the small field beyond the hotel grounds, his grey head—which always seemed too large for his body—resting on the top bar of the wooden gate, his great, sad eyes staring ahead, his ears drooping a little, either with age or weariness. Sara had bought him, years ago, for Adrian, when the old donkey-man on the St Cloe beach finally gave up.

'Methuselah, you funny old darling! It's me again.' Averil put an arm round his neck and stroked his wiry nose with her other hand. She was sure he recognised her; anyway, his eyelids with their absurdly long lashes drooped almost coyly, which made her laugh with delight.

'Oh dear, and I've forgotten to bring your carrots— what a shame! Look, have a sup of grass.' She pulled up a tuft by the roots and waved it beneath the old donkey's nose, but he averted his head pointedly. She waved again on the other side, but Methuselah wasn't going to be tempted.

'Probably grass hasn't much novelty value,' said a man's deep voice behind her. 'Does he care for sugar lumps?'

She spun round to meet a pair of very dark blue eyes fixed on her with a steady kind of flicker. She'd know those eyes anywhere, she thought. Her knees had gone weak again, but she held on to the top of the gate and managed a commendably ordinary tone of voice. 'Sugar lumps are Methuselah's version of ambrosia from heaven.'

He had taken a couple of sugar lumps from his pocket and was unwrapping them. 'You'd better offer them. He might take exception to a stranger.'

He put the lumps into her outstretched palm for a split second their hands touched and something like an electric shock ran up her arm. She spun out the business of feeding the sugar to Methuselah as long as she could, but eventually she had to turn and meet those

34

blue eyes again.

He regarded her silently for a lengthening moment, then he said, 'So we were speeding towards the same destination after all!'

He *did* remember her, then. Suddenly tension relaxed and she smiled demurely. '*You* were speeding. I was doing a very correct thirty-five.'

'Not all that correct! I seem to remember a certain blue Mini wandering very incorrectly into the middle of the road just when I was about to pass.'

'I didn't—' she began indignantly. Then habitual honesty took over. 'Yes, I know. I'm sorry.'

He raised his eyebrows. They were dark well-marked eyebrows, growing to a point in the middle of each, which gave him a faintly devilish appearance. 'A woman driver who admits she was at fault! Well, well!'

'I haven't been any sort of a driver very long,' she said, 'and anyway, why not admit you were wrong if you were? I think the war of the sexes is a waste of time.'

'Make love, not war, you're saying? My own sentiments exactly!' He grinned wickedly down at her.

She flushed. The conversation was getting a trifle out of hand. She said, ignoring that last quip, 'You must be Mr Randall. I'm Averil North, Mrs Tyndall's sister.'

He nodded, his eyes resting on her face with undisguised pleasure. 'Yes, I know. I asked her just now, and she told me you were staying with her here for a few days. That might make all the difference.'

'Difference—to what?'

He didn't answer straight away. He leaned against the gate, hands in pockets, causing Methuselah to back away nervously. Then the old donkey approached again and nuzzled his head between the bars towards the pocket of the burgundy red jacket. 'He learns quickly, doesn't he?' the man said. 'I'll see what I can find, old chap.' He produced another sugar lump, and this time he offered it to Methuselah himself. 'I don't take sugar in my tea,' he explained to Averil, 'so I always keep the spare lumps. You never know when they'll come in handy. I once rode a camel who wouldn't budge an inch without them. Now, what was I saying? Oh yes, it would make all the difference to me if you were staying here for a few days.'

Gaiety suddenly bubbled inside her. Even if he were an outrageous charmer—which he certainly was —he was fun. Anything less like the picture Sara had painted of him she couldn't imagine.

'I understood from my sister that you were here on company business, Mr Randall,' she said.

'Ah, that!' He looked thoughtful. Then, 'You were on your way somewhere?'

'I was going to walk down to the sea.'

'Let's both go down to the sea, then. And as we're both connected with the same company, won't you call me Bill? And perhaps you'd spare me a little of your time to point out the interesting features around here. I'm a stranger in these foreign parts.'

'You won't find any camels here,' she said. She felt as if she had drunk several glasses of champagne. As they fell into step together in the narrow lane she had a strong desire to put her hand through his arm. It seemed quite unbelievable that they had seen each other for the first time only about an hour ago. She seemed to have known him all her life.

About fifty yards on, the lane took an abrupt turn and the sea appeared spread out before them, very blue under the April sky, and flecked with white here and

there. On either side rose the granite cliffs of Cornwall, enclosing a tiny cove, far below, to which steps,
carved out of the rock, led down. A small boat was
pulled up on to the beach, and a few gulls strutted
about; otherwise the cove was empty.

Bill Randall leaned his forearms on the wooden
safety rail at the top of the steps and looked down.
'Nice,' he said. 'I'm beginning to think that this
assignment may turn out much more enjoyable than
I'd expected.'

That sounded like a loaded remark, but she hesitated to follow it up. If Sara were right about him—
she didn't think Sara *was* right, but she had to admit
the possibility—then she ought to watch her step with
this man until she had had time to make up her mind
about him.

She said, 'I love it here. I never get tired of coming
back.'

'You used to live here?'

'When my father was alive. He took over the management of the Cormorant when he left the Navy, and
my sister helped him. When he died she took his
place. That's why she's so good at the job; she learned
it all from the inside. I think that's the best way, don't
you?'

'I'd say it was the best way to learn anything,' he
said. Averil felt a little surge of relief at his words.
Surely if Ravens expected their managers to be pro-
ducts of a formal training college he wouldn't have
said that?

'So—your sister stayed and you left. Where did you
get to?'

'Exeter,' she told him. 'Not so very far away. I
went there to art school.'

'I'd never have taken you for an artist.'

37

She laughed. 'I'm not a real artist. I liked doing things with my hands, and I finished up making jewellery.'

'Diamond tiaras?'

'Heavens, no, nothing like that. Very humble really.'

'Interesting,' he said, and he really sounded interested, not just polite. 'I'd like to see some of it.' He glanced down at her hands. 'That's not one of yours, is it?'

She was wearing a ring on the third finger of her right hand, an intricate leaf pattern in beaten copper with delicate silver veins and stem. 'Yes, that's my latest effort.'

He took both her hands and held them lightly in his, looking down at them. It was crazy how her heart began to thump in her throat. Even out here on the cliff, with the breeze blowing gustily off the sea, she thought he must hear her heartbeats. She was glad she had spent a lot of time and effort keeping her hands and nails in good order. They were nice hands, slim and fine-skinned, with sensitive fingertips; but working in metal—cutting, filing, soldering, polishing— meant that she had to be scrupulous in her care.

He held her hands a moment longer, then he grinned up at her. 'Beautiful,' he said, and she knew he wasn't only referring to the ring. 'I'm glad the ring is on your *right* hand.'

There wasn't anything wrong with that, the way he said it, lightly, laughingly, openly admiring. She got the impression that he was a man who wouldn't waste any time in going after what he wanted, but it didn't fit in at all with Sara's idea of him as underhand and cunning, sent here to spy on her and report to head office.

Suddenly she was impatient with this whole situation. She had always hated anything devious and underhand, and now she wanted all cards on the table. She wanted to tell him straight out, at the beginning of their acquaintance, what Sara suspected, and hear him laughingly deny it. But of course she couldn't. It wasn't her game, it was Sara's, and Sara never put all her cards on the table these days. She used to be sweet and trusting and open, but not any more, and after what had happened you couldn't really blame her.

Averil turned to the sea, holding on to the wooden rail as the breeze cooled her hot cheeks and flipped up strands of hair escaping from the green scarf. 'Why did you have to come here?' she said. That at least she could ask.

'That doesn't sound awfully complimentary.'

'No, I meant—you said you wanted to be somewhere else.'

'Oh, that!' He paused for a moment, then said enigmatically, 'The clock struck twelve. I'm not a very convincing Cinderella, nevertheless that was roughly the position. You see—'

A sound from behind made them both turn, to see Lily, the little maid from the village, running across the grass, panting. 'Mr Randall! There's been a phone call for you from London, sir, and I was to say you're to ring back.' She paused for breath and added, 'It was Mr Raven, Mrs Tyndall said.'

'Damn,' said Bill with such feeling that Lily goggled, and her mouth began to tremble. 'I'm s-sorry, sir—' she quavered.

Bill looked at her quickly. 'I didn't mean you. Thank you for coming to tell me.' He gave the child a smile which obviously rocked her back on her heels.

She gazed at him for a moment, then, bright crimson, turned and scuttled away.

Bill Randall heaved a deep, exaggerated sigh. 'I'd better go, I suppose. One mustn't disobey the fairy godmother. See you.'

She stood and watched him stride up the lane and again she thought how easily he moved, like an athlete. You couldn't see him as an executive, sitting behind a desk. At the corner he turned and lifted a hand and she waved back, buoyantly glad that he seemed to be as much aware of her as she was of him. He was gay, exciting, and his personality matched her mood exactly. After months of wondering whether she could ever turn herself into the kind of person Kevin wanted her to be, she felt she was ready for a bit of excitement, perhaps even a flirtation. If the thought that, with Bill Randall, she might be playing with fire occurred to her, she wasn't troubled by it. At the moment she felt very much alive, even a little reckless.

She stretched up her arms and the breeze whipped her face and the white horses tossed on the waves and the gulls swooped and soared, and she had never felt so alive as at this moment.

She turned back towards the hotel, wondering which, of the two dresses she had brought with her, she should wear for dinner.

Finally she decided on the dress in an Aztec pattern, with a long, swishy skirt which flattered her ankles, which, she knew, were very nice ankles indeed. The colours of the dress were flattering too: orange and leaf green and brown. She brushed her hair until it lay against her neck like russet-coloured satin, and when she had taken a final satisfied look in the mirror, she ran downstairs, dithering a little inside with happy anticipation.

There was nobody about at the front of the hotel, so Averil went straight through to the back quarters. Here all was pre-dinner activity, but there was no rush or hectic bustling about. Mrs Bulteel, who had been cook at the Cormorant ever since Averil could remember, wouldn't have stood for that. She was a large, solidly-built woman, and as she moved from stove to working surface, and back again with deliberate steps, Averil thought that no Italian chef supplied by Ravens could have been more imposing. She wore a spotless white coat and her hair was hidden beneath a cap of stiffened cotton that was a compromise between a chef's tall hat and a Scottish tam-o'-shanter, and as she stirred here and tasted there she looked supremely in charge of the situation. Lily and another girl in waitress's uniform were piling dishes and a third girl was busy at the sink. Delicious savoury smells came from the great soup pan on the stove, and a gentle hissing and crackling from the direction of the grill.

Averil, who knew better than to intrude into the kitchen at this critical period of the day, hovered in the background. Presently Sara caught sight of her and came across. 'Everything's under control and I'm not needed any more. Come along and meet the Bartrams, if they're about. You know Miss Stevens, don't you? She was here when you came at Christmas.'

In the short passage to the hall Sara gave her sister an appreciative glance. 'You look very pretty, love. New dress?'

'Um, I splashed out on it last week. I'm christening it in your honour.' But to herself she admitted that that wasn't strictly true, and as they reached the front of the house her heart fluttered as she thought that at any moment she might see a tall, lithe masculine

41

form and a pair of very dark blue, amused eyes.

Just before they reached the lounge Sara said under her breath, ' By the way, the Randall man won't be in for dinner, praise be. He had a phone call and said he had to go to meet a friend in Truro, and he would probably dine there. Suits me! Ah, the Bartrams are here. Come along, and I'll introduce you. Mrs Bartram, Colonel Bartram, this is my sister Averil North—' She smiled and went back to the kitchen.

It was strange how you could meet people and talk to them and yet not really be there at all. It was moments before Averil surfaced from the depths of disappointment into which Sara's words had plunged her, and it was the sound of the dinner gong that brought her back. Mrs Bartram, a thin little woman with white hair, was smiling amiably. Her husband, the Colonel, towered above her, silent but benign. Thankfully Averil decided that she couldn't have said anything wildly out of place.

' —I really don't know how she does it,' Mrs Bartram was saying in a soft, precise voice. ' I think she's a very clever girl, your sister, Miss North. And everything is so beautifully kept—' She waved an arm around the lounge, and indeed, Averil thought, she was right. The chintz covers and curtains were impeccable; the oyster grey carpet was spotless; the furniture glowed with a dull sheen and emitted a faint aroma of lavender polish. ' —and the food is excellent too,' continued Mrs Bartram enthusiastically. ' So well cooked and such variety! We have been in hotels all over the world, but this one could hold up its head with any. Aren't I right, Hugh?'

The Colonel smiled faintly beneath his moustache. ' Quite right, my dear, quite right.'

Averil murmured something appropriate. Well!

she thought, Sara could certainly apply here for a glowing reference if she needed one. She wondered if she could get Mrs Bartram to give a repeat performance in Bill Randall's presence.

Miss Stevens appeared in the lounge doorway then, and the Bartrams drifted off into the dining room.

Averil liked Miss Stevens. She was a tall, quiet, intelligent woman in her sixties, with pretty, fading hair and a straightforward manner. Until her retirement she had been headmistress of a large girls' grammar school in the home counties. Soon after she retired she had had to undergo a severe operation, and now she was making a long stay at the Cormorant to recuperate before taking up new work for a charity trust.

She greeted Averil with pleasure. ' How nice to see you again, my dear! Your sister has given me news of you now and again. I'm sure she will be delighted to have you with her for a stay. And how is the jewellery-making getting along? Is business good?'

' Booming, thank you.'

' That's splendid. You must tell me all about it after dinner.'

Averil promised she would, and, as it turned out, she spent most of her evening chatting to Miss Stevens and the Bartrams in the lounge. All of them, it appeared, preferred her company to watching TV, and, as Sara had disappeared into her office to work, it was pleasant to sit round the big fireplace in the lounge, with its crackling logs, and chat to Miss Stevens and Mrs Bartram, while the Colonel sat with his pipe, silent but nodding occasionally with his quiet smile. It was after ten o'clock when she finally left them and went to look for Sara.

In the office her sister raised weary eyes from the

array of books and papers before her. 'V.A.T.,' she explained, waving a deprecating hand towards them. 'I'm expecting the accountant any day. I do hope you didn't mind my disappearing, love, but you seemed quite happy with the guests, and they were obviously loving nattering to you, so I thought I'd get on with all this. But I'll pack it in now.'

'Not because of me,' Averil said. 'Finish off, if you want to.'

'Sure you don't mind? Well, I will, then. Give me another quarter of an hour and then we'll have a cosy drink of something hot before we turn in.' She frowned. 'Has the Randall man come back yet, do you know?'

'I haven't really noticed,' Averil said, so casually that she felt a hypocrite. She knew quite well that if he had come in she would have been aware of it from the moment he came inside the front door.

'I hope he won't be too late, and keep Bulteel from his bed, waiting to lock up. I don't suppose Mr Randall would even consider that. No doubt Raven Hotels provide an all-night porter, together with their other VIP service.'

Averil raised her eyebrows. 'You really *have* got a down on the man, haven't you, Sal? It's not like you to sound so vindictive.'

'I just don't like him,' Sara said in a tone so harsh that her sister hardly recognised it. Then, suddenly, she relaxed and smiled and was herself again. 'Don't take any notice of me, love. I'm just edgy at present, that's all.'

Averil hesitated a moment, looking at the elder girl's worried face. Then she leant forward and patted her sister's hand. 'Cheer up, it'll all come right, Sal.'

Sara looked startled. 'That's what Father always

used to say. I'd forgotten.'

'It's true, you know. It works if you believe it. I'll go out and have a breath of air in the garden. Give me a call when you've finished.'

Averil collected her coat, slung it round her shoulders, and wandered out into the garden. It was a lovely evening. The breeze had gone down with the sun, and the air was still and cool and full of the earthy spring smell of growing things. The lawn cushioned her feet and tiny creatures in the flower bed kept up their incessant chirping. High above her head the dark plumes of the palm trees were etched against the sky, palely lit by a quarter-moon.

She drew in a deep breath of pleasure. This was the only home she could remember and she loved every bit of it. She understood Sara's feelings only too well. And Sara had so much more to lose than just her home —security for Adrian as well as for herself. It was probably quite true what she said, that she would never get another job like this one.

At the end of the garden you could catch glimpses of the sea between the high sheltering rocks. It was smooth now, a dull metallic silver gleam in the moonlight. Averil stood leaning on the stone wall, drinking in the peace of it. Surely, surely, this place was perfect enough as it was? Surely even Raven Hotels wouldn't want to change it? But what if Sara was right, and Bill Randall was here to examine and assess, with a view to turning the Cormorant into just another plushy, five-star retreat for tired executives? They might even want to pull down the whole place and rebuild. She spun round as if to reassure herself that the old house was still there, which it certainly was.

Then she suddenly became very thoughtful indeed. If she herself were entertaining such dark suspicions, in spite of her brave reassuring words to Sara, there was only one thing to be done, and that was to find out the truth. And there was only one person from whom she could find out the truth, and that person was Mr William Randall himself.

She squared her shoulders unconsciously. She was certainly no Mata Hari, the beautiful spy, but surely she could find out enough about Ravens' intentions to clear away that worried frown from Sara's brow. Anyway, she could try.

Right on cue came the purr of a car engine, the flash of headlights, from round the front of the hotel. Averil's pulses leapt nervously and she had a ridiculous urge to stay where she was, in the shadowy depth of the garden; but shyness wouldn't get her anywhere with the sophisticated Mr Randall, so she drew in a deep breath and strolled back up the lawn and round to the front entrance with what she hoped was an appearance of complete composure.

Bill Randall was standing in the hall, looking up the staircase. He turned round when he heard her come in, a gleam of what might have been pleasure in his eyes. 'Hullo there, I was just wondering if everyone retired at an early hour in these foreign parts. I've had to meet a train in Truro and drive a colleague up to the north coast, but I didn't want to keep the staff up late. I should have asked for a key, probably.'

'Oh, you haven't kept anyone up. My sister's still working in the office.'

He looked horrified. 'Working? At eleven o'clock at night?'

'There's a great deal of paper work to do,' she said, and then wished she hadn't said it. Would he assume that Sara was inefficient because she couldn't get through what she had to do in the space of an ordinary working day?

'Doesn't she have a secretary? I thought all hotel managers had secretaries.' He looked genuinely puzzled.

'No, she doesn't.' Averil had no intention of being drawn into a discussion about the staffing of the Cormorant. That was a matter between him and Sara.

'H'm we'll have to see about that,' he said thoughtfully.

At that moment Sara's head appeared round the corner of the passage. 'You there, Averil? Cocoa's laid on in the kitchen.'

She came further into the hall, and only then saw Bill Randall standing beside the door of the telephone room. She seemed to stiffen, and her expression changed immediately to the formal one she reserved for new guests. 'Oh, you're in, Mr Randall. Can I get you a drink?'

He nodded, smiling. 'I'd love one. I'm very partial to cocoa myself, if you've got a cup to spare.'

Sara stared at him briefly, in a way that made Averil feel uncomfortable. Then she said, 'Certainly. I'll bring a cup into the lounge for you.'

He strolled towards her across the hall. 'Hey, what's wrong with the kitchen? I'm one of the firm, remember? I don't rate special treatment. As a matter of fact it's a very comfortable kitchen; I've located it already. I always make a point of locating the kitchen wherever I happen to be staying—in case I want to raid the fridge in the wee small hours. Would you mind?' He grinned at Sara in the friendliest way.

Surely, Averil thought, she would unbend a little now. It was obvious that the man was going out of his way to be pleasant.

But Sara didn't unbend. She glanced at him coolly

and said, ' Of course, you must do just as you like, Mr Randall.'

She turned and led the way to the kitchen and Averil followed unhappily, not looking at Bill, beside her.

To her, a going-to-bed cup of cocoa was a kind of family ritual—a time of warmth and laughter and confidences shared, irritations talked out and usually dissolved. It could have been like that now, she thought, if only Sara hadn't been so—so full of unfounded suspicions. She seemed to be going out of her way to get on the wrong side of Bill Randall. If she had *wanted* to antagonise him she couldn't have gone about it in a more obvious way.

She stole a look up at him now and felt a quick pang of something like fear, because he wasn't smiling any more. His mouth was a straight line, and he looked like a man whom it would be unwise to snub.

Oh dear, thought Averil dismally, this was going to be the most unenjoyable cups of cocoa she had ever drunk.

CHAPTER III

The cocoa-drinking ceremony was not a success. Bill Randall, suddenly silent and looking rather grim, drank his cocoa standing up. Averil racked her brains for something to say that would restore the friendly atmosphere which had been there before Sara appeared, but could think of nothing, and the silence lengthened awkwardly. Finally he put down his empty mug on the kitchen table and said, ' Thanks for the drink, Mrs Tyndall. Perhaps we can get together over the books tomorrow morning?'

' Of course.' Sara was coolly polite. ' Any time that

48

will suit you.'

'Right,' he said in the same tone. 'Goodnight, then.'

For a moment he stood there, across the table from them, hands thrust into his pockets, frowning faintly as he looked at the two girls sitting together. Averil got a curious feeling that this was some sort of encounter, and that she was on Sara's side, lining up against him. Quickly she pushed back her chair and got up to take her cocoa mug to the sink. When she turned round he had gone.

Sara was still sitting at the table, and Averil came towards her, bursting out impulsively, 'Sal, why on earth do you have to be so—so distant with him? It's not like you to be prejudiced. Anyone would think you *wanted* to talk yourself out of a job, and—'

She stopped. Sara wasn't listening to her. Her forearms were folded along the table and her head was drooping on to them with sheer fatigue.

Averil was immediately filled with remorse. She leaned down and put an arm round Sara's shoulders. 'You're whacked, girl. Off to bed with you this moment. I'll wash up the mugs and see all the lights are turned out.'

Sara lifted her head as if it were too heavy for her. A strand of dark hair fell over her forehead and the blue veins showed at her temples through skin that was almost too delicate and transparent. 'But we were going to talk. I want to hear about the studio—and all you've been doing—'

'Tomorrow,' Averil said firmly. 'At this present moment you need sleep and lots of it. Go along with you now. No arguing!' She knew when Sara had reached the end of the road; she had seen it happen before. She pulled her to her feet. 'Upstairs now,

49

that's an order.'

Sara grinned feebly. 'Bully! All right, I will, then. I do feel a bit tired. Would you like a hot bath before you turn in?'

'Yes, I'd love one. But don't, for heaven's sake, stay awake for me, will you?'

Sara yawned. 'I don't believe I could—not even for you. I'll go up the back stairs, then. Will you make sure everything's locked up in front, and the lights out? I told Bulteel he needn't wait.'

When she had gone, Averil washed the cocoa mugs, made sure the kitchen was tidy for Mrs Bulteel in the morning, and went into the hall. The lounge was in darkness and the door partly open. Bill Randall had evidently gone up to his room; the other three guests had gone up earlier. Just then the small chiming clock in the dining room tinkled out eleven, and at that moment she remembered. Heavens! She had promised to give Kevin a ring this evening, and she had never given it a thought until now.

She hesitated outside the door of the telephone room. It was rather late for a casual phone call and Kevin had probably forgotten anyway. Still, she *had* promised. She went in and dialled the number of his flat in Exeter.

He answered immediately. 'Averil? At last! I was just going to ring you. Are you all right? I was getting quite worried.' He sounded faintly reproach-ful.

'I'm quite all right, Kevin. I had a splendid run down here; no trouble at all. Sorry I didn't ring earlier, but I got caught up in the social scene here.' She grinned to herself, remembering the chilly little episode which had just taken place in the kitchen. 'We all got talking after dinner and you know how the time goes.' There was no reason why she should justify herself to Kevin, but she felt a trifle guilty that he had, apparently, been sitting by the phone waiting for her to ring.

'Oh well—so long as you're all right!' He still sounded aggrieved. 'I wasn't at all happy about that car of yours.'

'She went like a bird all the way. How's business been today?'

Kevin was always willing to talk about his art boutique, and he did so now—at length. The new line in pottery was going splendidly, he said, and the thonged leather belts were a good selling line. '—and I sold two of those brooches of yours, the silver and coral ones, to some Americans. They seemed quite taken with them. You'll have to do some more like that for me when you get back. Have you decided which day you will come back, dear?'

That 'dear' sounded decidedly proprietorial, and she wasn't at all sure she liked that. 'I haven't thought about it yet. I've only just got here.'

She made that light and joking, but he replied quite seriously, 'Then *do* think about it. This place is ghastly without you. I could come down next Sunday and we could drive back together. Then I could keep an eye on—'

'Oh no, Kevin,' she broke in quickly. 'I mean, I may stay on into next week, I really don't know. So it wouldn't be worth your coming all this way just for an hour or two. I'll let you know when I make up my mind.' There was a short silence and she thought she had probably hurt his feelings. 'I promise I'll let you know,' she said again.

'Well, I suppose I'll have to be satisfied with that. You won't forget?'

'No, of course not. I must go now, Kevin, Sara has asked me to lock up. Good night.'

She didn't exactly hang up on him, but she didn't give him the chance of going on talking either. She replaced the receiver and stood looking at it thoughtfully. She had an uncomfortable feeling that she was being rushed along too quickly into something she wasn't at all sure about.

She had known Kevin Bryant for about three months, since the day she had walked into his art boutique to try to enlist him as a buyer, or at least an agent, for her jewellery. He had seemed to like her work (which, she admitted frankly to herself, had attracted her towards him from the start) and that had been the beginning. Until quite recently their association had been almost entirely one of friendly business. Then, one day, he had asked her opinion about some changes he was contemplating in the boutique, and she had gone there that evening to talk about it.

After that they had drifted into the habit of seeing each other every day. She had lost touch with most of her art school friends, who had taken jobs in other towns, and she had been working too hard establishing herself in her studio to make new friends just at present. Kevin was knowledgeable about her work and she enjoyed talking to him. Soon it seemed to be taken for granted that he would wander along to her studio when the boutique was closed for the day. She would cook a meal for them both and they would listen to records, or occasionally go to a cinema. One Sunday he had driven her into the country for the day.

There hadn't appeared to be anything romantic about it. Just lately Kevin had taken to kissing her when they said goodnight, but he didn't seem to be any more carried away by their kisses than she was, and certainly nothing had been hinted about a possible future together. Now that they were apart, it seemed, he was missing her more than she would have expected.

Frowning faintly, she went out into the hall, tested the lock on the big front door, and switched out the lights, so that everything was in darkness except for the glow from the landing above.

Then she saw Bill Randall standing in the lounge doorway, at the far end of the hall, silhouetted by the pale moonlight behind him, and her heart gave a jump and then started a crazy tattoo. 'I—I thought everyone had gone to bed—'

'I heard your voice on the phone,' he said, crossing the hall to her. 'So I waited.'

'I put the light out—' Her laugh sounded high and squeaky.

Her hand went up to the switch, but he stopped her, his fingers warm over hers. 'I've been enjoying the view of the garden by moonlight. Don't spoil it. You know, I'm beginning to be quite fascinated by this place. Just come and look.' He put his hand at her elbow and urged her towards the wide window in the lounge. The moon had risen high now, transforming the whole garden—the grass, the flower beds, the palm trees—to silver. In the distance the sea was a wide silver band against the darker sky.

Bill Randall said quietly, 'Yes, I like this place. I like everything about it. I like your sister too— although she doesn't like me.'

What could you say to that? Averil made a small, non-committal noise, and in the faint light she could see his smile. 'A pity about that,' he said. 'I shall have to try to make her change her mind.'

'You don't waste any time, do you?' she said. 'Do

you always go straight to the point like this?'

'Always. I go on the principle that a thing which has to be manœuvred and manipulated isn't worth having. Now then, where are you going to take me tomorrow afternoon, when I've finished a morning's work?'

'I don't know if—' she began. She had always liked people to be direct, but this man took her breath away.

'You're not booked to do anything else?'

'No, but—'

'Fine, then we'll start out about two, shall we, and go where the spirit moves us?' He was standing very close behind her and now he put his hand on her shoulder and gave it a small squeeze. 'Say yes.'

She laughed helplessly. 'Yes.'

He laughed too and she liked the sound of his laugh. *You're wrong about him, Sara,* she thought, *he's genuine. He's not putting on an act of being friendly for dark reasons of his own.*

'Good,' he said. 'Now I'll let you go to bed.' For a moment his grip hardened on her shoulder and then he let her go. When he took his hand away she felt curiously lost.

'I promised I'd see things were all right down here,' she said, hesitating.

'*I'll* do that. Everything locked up. Lights out. That the drill?'

'Yes, but why should you—'

'There you go again! I'm on the staff too. Don't you believe me?' His tone was faintly mocking.

'Yes, of course,' she said. She had meant it to sound light, but it came out oddly solemn, almost like a confession of faith. She turned away from the window, but he didn't immediately move to let her pass and she could see his face in the moonlight, half in shadow, his eyes fixed on her. And suddenly the atmosphere was supercharged; she imagined she could hear the crackle of the volts that jumped the gap between them.

'You'd better go, hadn't you?' he said very softly, and stepped back. 'Goodnight, Averil.'

'Goodnight,' she murmured, and she turned and ran up the stairs towards the lighted landing.

Next morning Averil wakened to find Sara dressed, standing in front of the mirror, putting finishing touches to her hair.

Averil stretched bare arms above her head luxuriously, her face turned to the sunlight streaming in through the window. 'Ooh—I slept like a log. What's the time?'

Her sister looked round. ''Morning, love. No hurry, it's only seven. Lily can't come in this morning, she has to go to the hospital with her mum, so I must be down early to lend a hand in the kitchen.' She tucked a strand of dark hair neatly behind her ear.

Averil sat up in bed, hugging her knees. 'Sal, what staff *have* you got at present?'

Sara turned quickly. 'Why?'

'Nothing, really, I just wondered. You seem rather bogged down with work yourself, and the season hasn't really started yet, has it?'

'Oh, you mustn't worry yourself about me, Averil. I'm fine. I went on a bit too long last night, that's all —nothing that a good night's rest hasn't put right.' And indeed, thought Averil, she did look much better this morning, which was reassuring.

Sara took off her frilly make-up cape and put it in a drawer. 'There *have* been a few staffing problems,' she said. 'I'll tell you about it when we get time for a chat. I've got to give this morning to the Randall man, it seems, but perhaps this afternoon—'

This was the moment to tell Sara about this afternoon; to say, quite casually, 'I've promised to go out with him myself this afternoon—he's asked me to show him round the coast.' But for some stupid reason she couldn't say the words, and then the opportunity had passed, for Sara was at the door. 'I must dash now, love. Come down when you're ready.'

Averil sat still when her sister had gone, her face thoughtful. She had never held out on Sara before, and she hated herself for doing it now. Sara was 'family' and she loved her dearly, and it was totally against Averil's nature to be evasive with anyone she loved. She told herself that it was a stupid little incident—not important at all, but she couldn't quite manage to believe herself. It seemed all the more urgent to find out, if she could, what exactly Bill was doing here, and to straighten out what she felt sure was a misunderstanding on Sara's part. This afternoon she would try to do just that.

Breakfast was served from half past eight onwards, and she was in the dining room promptly. None of the visitors was down yet, and Sara was busy in the kitchen, so Averil sat alone at the small staff table near the communicating door into the kitchen.

Joan's red head appeared round the door and Averil smiled at her. 'It's only me, Joan. Am I too early?'

'No, o' course not, Miss Averil.' Joan had worked for Sara since she left school, a year or so ago, and was an old friend. 'What would you like? Bacon and egg? Sausage?'

'Nothing cooked, thanks. Just some toast and coffee if you can rustle it up for me.' She usually ate a hearty breakfast at the Cormorant, but this morning she was ridiculously anxious to have finished and be out of the way before Bill Randall came down. By gulping down her second cup of coffee she managed to do it, and escaped upstairs.

She knew what she intended to do with her morning, while Bill was occupied with Sara, and now she checked her make-up carefully, pulled her green woolly coat over slacks and jersey, and ran down the back stairs. A glance into the long kitchen showed her that Sara was busy at the other end of it, but Joan was approaching with a laden tray.

Averil signalled to her and she stopped. ' Joan, my sister's busy, so I won't butt in just now. Would you tell her that I've taken the car up to the garage in the village to have a job done, and that I'll be back for lunch?'

' I'll do that,' Joan promised cheerily, hitching up her tray and applying a skinny hip to the swing door into the dining room. As it opened and swung back again Averil had a quick glimpse of the table for two in the far corner of the room; of a dark head turned to look out of the window, and a pair of very broad shoulders in a navy blue sweater. Her heart fluttered crazily and she fled out through the back door and round to the Mini at a most undignified speed.

Up at the garage Tom Berry was delighted to see her. Yes, he'd have a look at the petrol gauge for her, with pleasure. She left the car with him and walked on, pausing several times to have a word with the cottage people, who all knew her and were eager for a chat. As for Averil, she was in no hurry and she enjoyed hearing the local news. Half an hour had passed before she came out of the village and into the lane that led to Eliot's cottage.

The shortest way to the cottage was across the sandy cove below the Cormorant and up the steep grassy cliff on the other side. The inland way made a wide detour along a narrow lane between high banks, and it was this way that Averil was going today. As she strolled along, the spring sunshine hot on her head and the larks trilling away out of sight, she tried to decide what she was going to say to Eliot. He wouldn't recognise her, of course, as the twelve-year-old school-girl who had once followed him about like a devoted puppy.

She glanced at her watch. It was barely ten o'clock yet, and it might be rather embarrassing for Eliot to have a strange young woman knocking at his front door so early in the morning—especially if he had a wife with him. She hoped fervently that he *hadn't* got a wife. From the much too off-hand way that Sara had mentioned his return Averil guessed that she was more shaken by it than she wanted to admit. It would be wonderful if there could be a happy ending for Eliot and Sara after all this time.

Averil was so entranced by contemplating this delightful idea that she came upon the cottage before she expected, and before she had made up her mind how to approach Eliot. And now there was no time, for there was Eliot himself, in a bright blue wind-cheater, pumping water from the old-fashioned hand pump into a red plastic bucket.

He stopped pumping and looked up as she stopped beside the gate. At first she thought he hadn't changed a bit, and then she noticed that his light brown hair had thinned decidedly, and the grooves from nose to mouth, which had always made him look like a very handsome monkey, had deepened. She smiled uncertainly. ' Hullo, Eliot.'

He turned on her the politely mystified look of someone who is greeted by an unknown stranger. Then uncertain recognition dawned. 'It wouldn't be—you're not Averil?' She had forgotten what a nice voice he had, light and warm and quizzical.

'The same,' she nodded gaily.

He crossed the yard and came through the gate. 'Well, well, this is wonderful!' He put both his hands on her shoulders. 'How you've grown!' he said, and laughed.

She laughed too, and they hugged each other affectionately, just as if she were still twelve years old.

'I didn't think you'd recognise me,' she said, as he pushed open the cottage door for her to go inside.

'My dear child! With that gorgeous hair of yours, and that cheeky little nose! They could belong to no other than Averil North. Now, sit yourself down and I'll make some coffee and you can tell me all your news.'

It was grand to be sitting again in the cluttered little cottage parlour, nattering away to Eliot. He wanted to know all that had happened to her in the past ten years: how many 'O' levels she'd passed, and whether she had eventually reached art school as she had planned.

'I made it,' she told him. 'Exeter, to start with, and then on to London to specialise in jewellery-making.'

'H'm, you must have been good.'

'Enthusiastic,' she said, 'that gets you just as far.'

She told him about the studio and about the slowly growing demand for her work. 'I've even been able to afford a Mini.' She took a sip of coffee and added slowly, 'Mostly so that I could come down here more often to see Sara.'

There was quite a silence. Eliot looked down at the hearthrug, and when he lifted his eyes again she saw he looked tired. 'I was shattered when I met her in the village,' he said quietly. 'I thought she looked—well, never mind that now. I thought she went to London after she married.'

'You haven't heard?'

'Nothing at all. She didn't seem to want to talk to me, and I—well, I couldn't pretend to be merely the old family friend and start asking questions. Things between Sara and me had once been on too deep a level to take that line with her. I suppose I might have found something out by some tactful probing around the village, but that didn't appeal to me either.' He grinned faintly. 'I sat around here all yesterday, wondering what I could do.'

Yes, Eliot *would* do that; he wasn't the pushing sort. Until you got to know him well he seemed rather unapproachable, but later on you found that he had a very deep, almost shy reserve.

'It's ten years, isn't it?' she said. 'Where shall I start?'

'At the beginning. Which was,' he added, 'the end as far as I was concerned. Or so I felt then.'

'Yes, I was only a kid, but I think I knew that. But you got over it—you married?'

'No,' he said.

'I'm glad,' she said, and they smiled at each other. That was the nice thing about Eliot, you didn't have to explain what you meant.

So she told him everything that had happened since he left: about the disastrous failure of Sara's marriage; about Adrian; about their father's sudden and unexpected death and Sara taking over the management of the Cormorant in his place. Even about the sale of the hotel to the Raven group, and Sara's fears for the future of her job.

At some time during her story Eliot filled his pipe

and began to draw on it, but he didn't interrupt her once. When she had finished he was silent for a long time, then he said slowly, ' I wish I'd known.'

' What would you have done?'

' I'd have come back to look after her,' he said simply, and she nodded. That was exactly what she would have expected him to do.

' Is it too late?' She couldn't help it if that were tactless. She just had to know.

He gave her a very wry look. ' Ten years is a long time. Such a long time to waste. I don't know, we'll have to see what happens.' And before she could think of any follow-on to that he said, ' And how about you, young Averil? I imagine the men queue up, don't they? One in particular?'

It was quite ridiculous, but the thought of Bill Randall was there at the front of her mind immediately, and she felt her cheeks grow hot.

Eliot was watching her quizzically. ' Have I got the bullseye?'

She pulled herself together. ' There isn't any queue.'

' Really? You surprise me. You've turned into a most bewitching young woman, Averil North.' His eyes passed admiringly over her trim figure and long graceful legs as she sat there in the old basket chair opposite him. ' You don't mean to tell me there isn't a young man in Exeter, pining for your return.' This was the old Eliot, teasing like an elder brother.

' Well, there's Kevin,' she said, because that seemed safe as a topic. ' He has a rather good art-boutique-cum-gallery in Exeter. But we're not engaged or anything.' she added hastily.

' Very wise,' he nodded. ' Getting married is a serious step, even in these casual days. Better to take

61

your time and be sure.'

'I couldn't agree more,' she said brightly. 'I'm quite happy as I am.' It was true too, though not exactly as she had implied. She was happy because she was going to spend the afternoon with Bill Randall. So happy it made her tremble inside to contemplate it. She changed the subject and enquired about Eliot's work. Was he still writing books about birds? Was that why he had come back to the cottage?

He told her that in a way it was. He was now working with a small unit which made films of nature subjects all over the world. 'I expect you've seen some of them on TV,' he smiled. 'Nature is booming these days; it would appear that people can't know enough about their world, all of a sudden. We're thinking of doing a film down here, and I've come on ahead to spy out the land and the sea, so to speak. We haven't decided what angle to concentrate on yet, but there's quite a lot of Nature around these parts, isn't there? I've been across to Starry Rock, and I'll swear there are more species there than when I saw it last. Like to come and have a look? The tide's out at present.'

'Love to, if you can lend me some gumboots. I don't fancy paddling at this time of the year—much too chilly.'

Starry Rock was something between a very large rock and a very small island, situated about five or six hundred yards from the mainland, and inhabited entirely by birds. At low tide it could be reached on foot, if you didn't mind wading through a couple of shallow channels, and this was what they did now. It was like old times, being with Eliot, and when they reached the rock Averil dropped back easily into the habit of slow cautious movement he had taught her years ago. Even so, their arrival caused a bit of a stir among the residents, but after a time the fuss subsided and the birds returned to their never-ending occupation of searching for food.

Eliot was a fascinating companion. He knew every bird—the dainty little sandpipers, the oyster-catchers with their long orange beaks, the turnstones pecking about among the seaweed, the gulls of various kinds that swooped and screamed, and perched in a lordly manner on the highest rocks.

'Oh, look, there's a cormorant,' Averil pointed out to sea. But Eliot shook his head.

'Too small,' he said. 'Must be a shag. That's interesting.'

For a time they were both silent, revelling in it all —the tang of the salt air on their lips; the crisp spring sunlight that turned the rocks to mysterious things of iridescent beauty crusted with tiny shellfish; the cries of hundreds of birds mingling with the crash and boom of the waves.

Suddenly Eliot got very excited. 'Golly, I believe it's a—where are my binoculars?' He peered through them. 'Yes, it certainly is. Marvellous!'

'Is what?' whispered Averil.

'A greater yellow-legs. Visitor from North America. I've never seen one here before. Look, isn't he a beauty?'

He passed over the binoculars and she saw the bird, on a distant rock, slim and graceful with its speckled back and white under-rump, its long upturned beak and stilt-like lemon-coloured legs. 'Beautiful,' she sighed.

He was looking very intent. 'Yes, I think I can see how to photograph him, if he's here for any length of time. We might make a hide there—'

He pulled out a pad and pencil and began to sketch the contours of the surrounding rocks. Averil sat down and waited, knowing that he had forgotten all about her. She still held the binoculars, and now she trained them across the wet sand in the direction of the hotel. From this distance she could see the squat chimneys, over the tops of the palm trees. A little below were the cliffs, grass-covered and sloping easily for a third of their height, then giving way suddenly to bare granite which dropped straight down to the rock-strewn beach below. It was beautiful and wild and sometimes rather frightening. She moved the glasses a little and saw the path, the field, and even Methuselah, a tiny toy donkey, standing motionless in his usual position by the gate. I must take him some more sugar lumps, she thought, and that reminded her again of Bill Randall.

'Good!' Eliot snapped the band round his note-book. 'That ought to be super, if we can manage it. We might even do a whole piece about visitors from abroad—spring, summer and autumn. I can't remember if that's been done already.' He stood up and took her arm to help her up. 'Thanks for coming. Averil, you must have brought me luck.'

The tide had turned and the sand was rapidly being covered; the channels were deep enough to reach almost to their knees. When they had scrambled up to the cottage Eliot said, 'Have lunch with me? I've got some super corned beef.'

She chuckled. 'I'd love to stay and cook you something, Eliot. I well remember how you used to forget to feed yourself, and I bet you haven't improved one tiny bit. But I promised Sara I'd be back for lunch, so I'd better get going. Besides,' she added casually, pulling off the gumboots, 'I'm bidden to entertain our Man from Head Office this afternoon. You know, I told you about him. He wants to be shown round the countryside.'

Eliot pulled a sympathetic face and she felt a fraud, but she could hardly admit that she was counting the minutes to two o'clock.

Eliot came to the gate with her. 'Thank you again for coming, Averil. I'll be seeing you very soon. I've—got to decide what's best to be done.'

She said goodbye and left him standing there, his thinning hair blowing in the breeze, his kind brown eyes deeply thoughtful. Whatever he decides, I hope he's right, she thought. There was no room and no time for any more mistakes.

Tom had the Mini ready for her, the petrol gauge duly functioning again. She paid him slightly more than he asked and drove back to the hotel. Sara was behind the reception desk in the hall, and gave her a rather expressive shrug, which Averil pretended not to notice.

'Got all your bookwork sorted out?' she enquired cheerfully.

Sara pulled a face. 'Too true we have.' She glanced over her shoulder and said in a low, exasperated voice, 'It was a complete waste of time. The Randall man is an utter phoney. I guessed he was as soon as I saw him, and now I'm convinced.'

'But, Sal, surely it's too soon to—'

Sara shook her head. 'I just know he is, that's all. Why, he's absolutely incredible. He pretends he's come here to learn the hotel business. Pretends he doesn't know a thing about it and wants to start at the bottom and find how it all works.'

'Well, maybe he does,' Averil insisted.

Her sister gave a hollow laugh. 'You're much too

trusting. I ask you, just look at the man. Look at that great expensive car of his, look at his clothes, his winter-sports tan, everything about him. Does he look the kind of man who would learn anything from the bottom up? Men like that start at the *top*, from the very first moment in their cradle. No, you don't tell me—' Sara was becoming quite heated and Averil felt it was time to interrupt.

' Well, maybe I'll be able to find out something more about him this afternoon.'

Sara stopped in the act of hanging a key on the rack behind the desk and turned round slowly. ' You don't mean—'

' He asked me last night if I'd go out with him this afternoon. He wants to see the countryside.'

' And you're going?'

' Why shouldn't I?' said Averil, smiling.

Sara seemed suddenly to droop. ' Of course, why shouldn't you? I'm sorry I said what I did about him. I didn't know—'

Averil laughed. ' Sal, *darling*! There's nothing to know. I'm going for a run in his car, that's all. And if he happens to say anything about why he's here and whether Ravens have any ideas about the future of the Cormorant—well, that would be all to the good. Wouldn't it be better to know rather than worry about it and fear the worst?'

' Yes, I suppose so.' Sara came from behind the reception desk and linked her hand in Averil's arm as they walked towards the office. ' Sorry again, love. I'm being an awful drip, aren't I? It's all been so sudden. A week or two ago everything seemed to be going along smoothly. Adrian was settling down at school. We were nicely booked here and the winter decorating and renovating was all finished up to date, and then—wham! I think,' she said slowly, 'I'm afraid of change, that's what it is. But you're right, and I'll try not to worry because it won't make any difference in the end. Now, tell me what you've been doing with yourself this morning.'

'I took the Mini up to Tom at the garage to have the petrol gauge fixed.' Averil paused. 'And I saw Eliot. We had quite a chat.'

'Oh, did you?' Sara spoke quickly and brightly as if she had anticipated this and rehearsed her reaction. 'How is he?'

'Still the same Eliot. He didn't seem to me to have changed a bit, except grown older like we all have.'

They were in the office now and Sara said, still in that bright high voice, 'Indeed we have. Well, I must get the laundry list checked before lunch.'

She sat down at the desk and began to leaf through a wad of papers. Averil stood silently, watching her. Then she said, 'He's *not* married, Sal.'

Sara had a very expressive face, but she had learned, through the years, to control it. Now only someone who knew her very well, as Averil did, would have noticed the sudden flicker of her eyelids, the slight relaxing of her lips in a little sigh.

'He told me he's working with a unit making nature films. He took me across to Starry Rock and we had a look at the birds there. It was lovely there this morning, fresh and sunny.'

Sara seemed to brace herself for an effort and said, with a funny little smile, 'I'm glad you saw him, Averil. But—don't get any ideas in your head about Eliot and me, will you? It's all over, you know.'

She picked up a pencil and began to make ticks on a long list of items. Averil looked at her, at her soft brown hair and creamy skin and the curve of her breast under the black jersey material of her dress, and thought that Sara ought to be happily married, not giving all the hours of the day to being a business woman. Oh, she did it efficiently and responsibly—probably too responsibly for her own good—but that wasn't the point. There was Eliot in his solitary cottage, sitting down to a lunch of corner beef, and here was Sara, checking laundry lists as if it were the most important thing in life. It was a shame.

But there was nothing to be done about it now. Sara seemed to have put up this high wall around herself and you just couldn't get over it. So with a sigh and a shrug Averil left her to her laundry list and went to tidy up for lunch.

In the bedroom she brushed out the tangles that the breeze had put into her hair; and when all the tangles were gone she went on brushing until it hung to her shoulders like chestnut satin. She pulled off slacks and sweater and put on a woollen oatmeal dress with a batik silk cravat in a red and gold print. She slipped her feet into pale kid buckled pumps. She began to renew her make-up.

She had come upstairs with her mind full of Sara and Eliot, but by now all she could think of was that very soon she was going to see Bill Randall again. It was idiotic, of course, at her age, but as she leaned to the mirror to put on her lipstick she felt a queer churned-up sensation inside, rather like going back to school after the holidays.

I'll have to be careful, she thought, in case Sara is right after all. Could it be possible that he really *was* being devious and insincere about his visit to the Cormorant? That in spite of what he had told Sara about wanting to learn the business he was really here to assess her and report about her to his head office?

It would be too stupid to let herself fall in love with a man who could behave like that. Anyway, who said anything about falling in love? Surely she could react in a perfectly normal way to an attractive man without immediately wondering if she were in love?

She put the top back on her lipstick and stood up with an air of determination. She would enjoy the afternoon and not get any ridiculous ideas in her head about a man she had only just met.

CHAPTER IV

'Well,' said Bill, bringing the big silver-grey Mercedes to a halt just before the crossroads outside the village, 'where are you going to take me to?'

'Am I the courier?' Averil smiled at him from the luxurious depths of the passenger seat. He had changed into a white polo-neck sweater of some thick silky material; with his tanned skin, dark hair and keen blue eyes he looked, she thought with an inward squiggle of pleasure, quite devastatingly attractive. 'I feel too lazy. Like a cat in the middle of a pure down cushion. I don't really want to do anything but curl up and purr.' She stroked the soft pale leather of the seat between them. 'Is it a new car?'

'Fairly, I believe. But it's not my car, you know. Belongs to my boss.'

'Mr Raven?'

'That's the bird. The Old Bird, everyone calls him.'

'Yes, I've heard that.' She looked down at her hands. This might be a chance to find something out. 'Are you—do you like working for him?'

'That's a good question. I've only just started, and I

haven't had time to find out yet.' He grinned at her, his dark blue eyes dancing. 'Ask me again in six months time.'

Well, that line of enquiry hadn't got her anywhere. 'In six months' time you will have gone your way and I mine,'she said lightly. 'Ships that pass in the night.'

'I wouldn't say that. It's a horrid thought anyway, so don't let's contemplate it. Come on, kitten, uncurl yourself and give me some directions. I'm a stranger in these parts.'

So Averil gave up trying to quiz him on Sara's behalf and settled down to enjoy the magic of the afternoon. And pure magic it was. She had never been driven in a car like this before; on the main road it gobbled up the miles effortlessly, and when they turned off into the lanes it idled along amiably.

It was ages since she had been on an expedition like this and she made the most of it, directing Bill to the places she knew and loved. They went to Veryan to look at the round houses first.

'Why round?' Bill enquired, interested.

'So there were no corners where the Devil could hide,' she told him, and he laughed and said it was no place for him then.

They drove on to Caerhays Castle, the Gothic-style mock castle, romantic and mysterious against the background of dark woods. They went down the long hill to Gorran Haven, busy preparing itself for the summer season, the tiny shops in the narrow hilly street filling their windows with tempting mementoes to lure the tourists' money.

'Kitsch!' remarked Averil, looking at a brooch made of bright yellow shells, 'but nice kitsch. I like that brooch.'

'I shall buy it for you, then,' announced Bill, and

70

when the shop door turned out to be locked he insisted on knocking so hard and so long that finally he succeeded in attracting the attention of the owner, who was delighted to welcome customers so early in the year. But Bill didn't give Averil the brooch, when they came out of the shop. He slipped the small paper bag into his pocket and said cheerfully, 'Where next?'

Next they called at Mevagissey, parked the car just outside, and walked down to the harbour, once busy as the headquarters of the pilchard fishing industry, but now, like most of the other villages, sprucing itself up for the invasion of the holidaymakers. They found a café open, overlooking the harbour, where they had tea and home-made scones and looked down at the assortment of craft in the water below. Two pleasure boats were being painted, and several trim sailing boats rocked and bobbed at anchor. At the quayside dinghies and miscellaneous small boats were tied up. There was only one rather ancient fishing vessel to be seen.

Averil sighed. 'It's very sad really.'

Bill helped himself to another scone and spread it with jam. 'What's sad?' he enquired, smiling. 'Personally I'm having a grand time.'

'I mean, it's rather sad that the old Cornwall is losing its character and turning into a tourist attraction.'

'It's the way of the world, you can't alter that. You have something to offer, and you offer it. And if they *have* to turn themselves into holiday resorts I think they're doing it jolly well. I'm most impressed with all I've seen.' He looked across the table at her and added, 'You're thinking that I *would* look at it like that, being in the hotel industry myself, aren't you?'

She flushed. 'I suppose I was, in a way.'

71

' But you won't hold it against me?'

He was fooling, of course, but she replied seriously, ' That all depends.'

His eyebrows went up. ' What does that mean, exactly?'

Here was her opportunity to introduce the subject of the Cormorant and perhaps to find out what he was doing there. But she couldn't do it. She couldn't spoil her lovely afternoon, even in Sara's interests. Anyway, she wasn't sure it would be in Sara's interests; in fact she was fairly sure that Sara, in her present mood, wouldn't thank anyone to interfere.

She looked up and saw that his blue eyes were regarding her very quizzically. ' Your face is an open book, Miss North,' he grinned. ' I bet I know exactly what you're thinking at this moment.'

' You couldn't possibly——' she began indignantly, feeling her cheeks becoming even hotter.

He leaned back in his chair. ' How's this, then? You were wondering how you could find out, on your sister's behalf, exactly what my brief is down here.'

She stared at him speechlessly and his grin widened. ' Right on target, I can see. Don't look so surprised, I haven't got a crystal ball or anything like that in my pocket. It's a very natural reaction in the circumstances.'

She found her voice. ' Well then, if you're so clever at guessing what I was going to ask you, how about providing the answer?'

He laughed aloud and at the sound the little waitress at the other end of the room jerked her head round. ' Oh, Averil, you're wonderful! I do like a girl who comes straight to the point.' He went on laughing, and half reluctantly she laughed with him.

' Although I don't really think it's funny,' she said

at last. 'And I don't suppose you would if you were Sara.'

He stopped laughing and looked rather hard at her. 'Tell me—this job at the Cormorant—does it mean a lot to your sister?'

'Yes, it does.' Sara was so ridiculously proud these days; she wouldn't want any pleading done on her behalf. And yet Bill Randall possibly held her future in his hands. It would be just plain foolish to be too squeemish about it. 'I don't suppose she would admit it, but I think it means pretty well everything to her: a home, an income, security for her small son. But something else too,' she went on more slowly. 'I think it means having a purpose in life.'

'Her husband? Is she a widow, or—?'

'He walked out on her when Adrian was just a year old.'

'I see,' he said quietly.

It was up to him now; she had said all she was going to say. He sat quite still, obviously turning over in his mind what she had just told him. His face had changed; he looked serious, almost stern. Until this moment she had thought of him as a man who took life pretty lightly and easily, but now she saw that she could be very wrong indeed. There was a hard strength in the line of his mouth, in his jaw.

He lifted his head and said, 'It's quite a point, isn't it? I don't want to shrug it off, but neither is this the moment to think about business. Look, how would it be if I told you that I will do my very best to see that your sister's position is looked after?'

'That's a promise?'

'A promise.' He stretched across the table and covered her hand with his, setting up a tingling through her whole body. She met his eyes for a second and then looked away, her heart hammering.

'Shall we—shall we take some sugar lumps back for Methuselah?' she suggested huskily.

'That,' he said gravely, 'is a very good idea.'

After tea they got back on to the main road and made for Fowey. Bill drove more slowly now and Averil laid her head back against the soft leather of the seat and revelled in the warm feeling of happiness that had settled inside her. It was a heavenly afternoon, one of those April days which pretend to be high summer. The sun shone and the sky was blue, with little white puffy clouds. The villages they passed through, with their cottages and flowers, were like jewels on a necklace.

In Fowey they lingered on the waterfront, among the seamen in their navy blue jerseys, with their mahogany brown faces. They watched a china clay ship moving gently up the river to its loading creek.

Bill was a wonderful companion. He was interested in everything and asked questions all the time. Fortunately Averil was able to answer some of them. She had learned the history of Cornwall at school, and she told him of the proud, fierce seamen of Fowey—the Fowey Gallants—who sent raiding parties to the coast of France throughout the Hundred Years War. She showed him the house where Sir Arthur Quiller-Couch lived and wrote his novels. They climbed up to the ruins of St Catherine's Castle and stood on the headland amid the gorse and were rewarded by the wonderful view of the sea coast and the countryside all around.

'It's been lovely,' sighed Averil, when at last they returned to the car and she leaned back in luxurious relaxation. 'I adore Cornwall. I could easily go along with the idea of settling down here for the rest of my life.'

He gave her a wry look from the driving seat. 'Don't remind me of those dreaded words.'

'What dr—?'

'Settling down.' He drew it out with exaggerated gloominess. 'People seem to have a nasty habit of expecting you to do it, at my advanced age of thirty-one years.'

'And you don't go along with that?'

He pursed his lips and looked thoughtfully at the back of the car standing in front of them in the car park. 'Let's say that up to now I haven't given the matter any serious thought.' The dark blue eyes narrowed and twinkled in her direction. '*You're* not a settling down girl, are you, Averil?'

She replied, equally lightly, 'I'd have to have notice of the question. Certainly, up to now I haven't given the matter any serious thought.'

He laughed aloud. 'Splendid. We'll get along fine, then.' He switched on the engine and glanced at his wristwatch. 'Back to the Cormorant, I'm afraid. I'd have liked to take you out somewhere to a dinner *à deux*, if the idea appealed to you, but I have to be at one of our hotels up on the north coast by seven. Business!'

'Oh!' she said, and as he backed the car and drove on to the road she was dismayed by the blank disappointment that settled inside her. As they drove smoothly along the white sunny roads she had to take herself firmly in hand. Just because she had had a lovely afternoon, and because she and Bill Randall seemed to get along so well together, it didn't mean that the magic would go on indefinitely.

They were back at the Cormorant altogether too soon for Averil, but when Bill opened the car door on her side and said, 'Shall we go and give Methuselah his share of the afternoon's goodies?' she cheered up again.

There was nobody about as they strolled together along the drive and down the lane. The old donkey was in his usual place, resting his head on the bar of the gate. 'You look somewhat browned off, old chap,' Bill observed, feeding him the sugar lumps. He rubbed Methuselah's ear. 'Did they make *you* settle down too, then? I bet you'd rather have seen a bit of the world. You'd like it up in the High Andes,' he added. 'You'd meet lots of your friends and relations there.'

'Donkeys in the High Andes—camels in the desert—where in the world *haven't* you been?' Averil enquired, leaning her arms along the top of the gate. She glanced up at him, wrinkling her nose. 'You can't go on dropping items like that into the conversation without making a girl curious.'

'I'm looking forward to telling you the story of my life,' he grinned. 'But it may take some time. Meanwhile there's only time now to say thank you for a delightful afternoon. I can't tell you how much I've enjoyed it.'

She twisted round from the gate and Bill's face was very close; she hadn't known it was so close. For a long, long moment they looked into each other's eyes. Then, inevitably, his mouth was on hers and his arms were holding her against him. The kiss went on and on and time stood still. When he let her go her knees were trembling and she couldn't say a word.

He kept one arm round her. 'That was meant to be just a thank-you kiss,' he said huskily. 'Blame yourself for being such a delicious morsel, Averil.'

She grinned shakily. 'What big eyes you have,
76

Grandmother!'

He smiled, stroking back the silky hair at her temples. 'Is that what you think of me—that I'm the original Big Bad Wolf?'

'Are you?'

His brows lifted. 'I might ask if you're Little Red Riding Hood. Are you?'

'Guileless and trustful? We—ell, I'm not so sure about that.'

Methuselah had had enough of this nonsense. He stuck his head between the bars of the gate and butted his shaggy grey nose between them. They both laughed and Bill gave him another sugar lump. Then they wandered back up the lane. Averil stole a look at Bill's face, but it told her nothing that she wanted to know. He looked just the same as he always did— easy, confident, entirely self-assured, a man who would always get what he wanted without too much trouble. A little spurt of anger shook her and she wished she had not been so eager to let him kiss her. She had gone into his arms with a readiness that disturbed her.

As they came in sight of the hotel she put her hand to her hair. 'I can't go in looking like this—'

'Or Sister Sara will be even more convinced that I'm the villain of the piece?' He didn't sound at all put out by the possibility.

'It isn't really funny,' said Averil shortly. 'I hate her to be bothered and worried.'

She looked up and saw Mrs Bartram and Miss Stevens in the sun lounge, their heads close together, and she touched her hair again. 'I—I think I'll go round the back way,' she said. She hesitated . . . 'Thank you for—for the afternoon—and the tea, and everything.'

'Thank *you*,' he said blandly, and stood there, his

hands in his pockets, watching her run off across the grass, with what might have been a speculative look in his eye.

Sara was up in the bedroom, changing into a softly-draped mink-coloured dress with a gold link belt.

'Nice,' said Averil appreciatively, sitting on the bed and admiring the back view. 'New?'

Her sister leaned forward to apply pale apricot lipstick. When she turned from the mirror Averil thought she looked somewhat different. The colour in her cheeks was natural and she had a less anxious expression. 'Not specially new,' she said. 'Mail order. That's the way I buy my clothes these days—all I have time for. Nice afternoon?' she enquired casually, too casually to be convincing.

'Yes, lovely.' Averil tried to sound matter-of-fact and thought how horrid that they should seem quite unable to be natural with each other at present. 'We did a sort of coastal tour, as far as Fowey and then back by the main road. Had tea at Mevagissey. Is that a new café, on the harbour? I don't seem to remember it.'

Sara put the top back on her lipstick. 'I wouldn't know, I haven't been there for ages,' she said absently. She stood up. 'Averil, I've changed your table for dinner. I shan't be having my meal until later on, so I thought it might be a good idea for you to join up with Miss Stevens. It was her suggestion, as a matter of fact. All right with you?'

'Yes, of course. Miss Stevens is a dear.' It would be nice to have someone to talk to at dinner, to take her mind off the empty chair at the corner table, where Bill Randall should have been sitting.

'Oh, and I nearly forgot.' Sara turned at the door.

78

'Eliot phoned and booked in for dinner. I could hardly refuse at this time of the season.'

Averil stared across the room at her. 'Refuse? Why on earth should you refuse?'

'Well—' Sara's colour deepened. 'Oh, I don't know,' she finished up almost crossly, and went out and closed the door with a little slam.

Averil raised her eyebrows at her own reflection in the mirror. Then she renewed her make-up, tidied her hair and went down to the dining room.

Averil and Miss Stevens were half way through dinner when Eliot put in an appearance. He had, Averil noticed, with affectionate amusement, tried hard to spruce himself up since this morning, and was wearing a shirt and tie with slacks and a tweed jacket; all of which had probably been bought as 'crease-resistant' but would have looked much better for an expert press. But his hair was brushed down carefully and his eyes were as warm and amused as ever as he saw her and lifted a hand in greeting before Joan shepherded him to a small table at the far end of the room.

Miss Stevens quirked an appreciative eyebrow at Averil. 'H'm, another new face! Our quiet little backwater is waking up indeed. First the devastating Mr Randall, and now—who might this be?'

'Name of Dunn,' Averil told her. 'He's a naturalist. He has a cottage on the headland.'

'Dunn. Not Eliot Dunn? He has written some excellent books on birds?'

'Yes, that's the one.'

Miss Stevens beamed. 'But how splendid! You must introduce me, my dear. I've been a fan of Mr Dunn's for some time. Birds are my abiding delight.'

So over coffee in the comfortable chintzy lounge

Eliot and Miss Stevens talked birds, while Averil listened and wished that Sara would put in an appearance. It had seemed obvious to Averil that Eliot had booked for dinner at the Cormorant more in the hope of seeing something of Sara than for the satisfaction of a well-cooked meal, although of course she couldn't be sure. But time was passing, the curtains were drawn, and Sara was still nowhere to be seen, while Eliot was swapping bird stories with Miss Stevens with every sign of pleasure and none of impatience.

Averil sighed and looked round the room, wondering if there were anything she could do about the matter. Since dinner the Bartrams had been engaged in one of their games of cribbage, but now, as she looked their way, she saw that something was wrong. The Colonel was slumped back in his chair, mopping his forehead with trembling hands, and his little wife was hovering anxiously beside him.

Averil went across the room to her. 'Is your husband feeling ill?' she said in a low voice. 'Can we do anything to help?'

Mrs Bartram grabbed her arm and led her a few paces away and whispered, 'I'm so afraid it's a recurrence of an infection he caught out East some years ago. The doctors warned me he might have trouble with it again, but it's quite a time ago and I was hoping—' She glanced over her shoulder, her face desperately worried. 'He was very ill then, he nearly—' She drew in a breath and squared her shoulders and said in a calmer tone, 'I think I must get him up to bed straight away, and if there is a doctor available, perhaps someone could telephone him and—'

'Yes, of course. I'll go and tell my sister what has happened, and we'll put hot water bottles in the bed straight away.'

Sara had evidently had her dinner on a tray in the office. Averil found her there, the tray pushed aside, her head bent over her account books.

She looked up. 'Is it anything important, love? I'm wildly busy just at the moment.'

Busy she might be, but she was making the most of it too—probably to avoid meeting Eliot. Averil wished she knew why. She said, 'It *is* rather important. Colonel Bartram has been taken ill and his wife's worried sick about him. Could we possibly get Dr French to come out here, do you think?'

Sara was on her feet immediately. 'Of course. I'll call him straight away. Would you ask Joan to fill a couple of hot water bottles and take them up.' She lifted the receiver from the phone on her desk. 'What shall I say to the doctor? Does Mrs Bartram have any idea what's wrong?'

'She says probably some tropical bug he caught out East some time ago.'

'That's not very explicit, is it? I shouldn't think Dr French is exactly an expert on tropical diseases. I wonder what—'

'Look, Sal, why not bring Eliot in to help on this? He's travelled pretty well all over the world. I bet he knows quite a bit about tropical bugs.'

Sara frowned, biting her lip. 'Do you think he would—? Yes, of course he'd help, how silly I am.' She looked uncertainly at Averil. '*You* go and ask him, there's an angel.'

Anyone would imagine *I* was the elder sister, Averil thought as she made her way back to the dining room. Poor Sal, she's as nervous as a kitten at the prospect of seeing Eliot.

Miss Stevens was standing in the lounge doorway.

Averil glanced into the room behind her and saw that it was empty. 'Mr Dunn—he hasn't gone, has he?'

'Oh no, he's being most helpful. He and Mrs Bartram between them have got the Colonel up to bed. Poor man, he really looked dreadful. Is there a doctor anywhere in the neighbourhood he could see?'

'The nearest is Doctor French, at Poltegan. It's rather in the wilds, though, and as far as we know he's single-handed, but I'm sure he'll come if he's in. Sara's trying to contact his house on the phone now.'

Eliot came down the stairs. 'We've managed to get him into bed, and his wife is coping for the moment.' He frowned. 'I don't like the look of him, though. These tropical things can be very nasty. Can we get a doctor?'

Averil nodded. 'Sara's trying to get in touch with Doctor French on the phone now. Go and have a word with her, Eliot, she's in the office. She needs some help.'

He gave her an odd look. '*My* help?'

'Why ever not?' Surely Eliot wasn't going to be silly, as well as Sara?

Perhaps he guessed what she was thinking, for he smiled wryly and said, 'If you say so, then,' and went across the hall towards the office.

Miss Stevens looked after him thoughtfully. 'Mr Dunn was telling me that he is an old friend of your family. How lucky he happened to be here just now! It's such a responsibility for a hotel when someone is ill and I'm glad your sister has a man to help her cope with this. She has more than enough to do here, even when things go smoothly, without being faced with something like this.'

Averil nodded. 'Yes, I'm very glad Eliot happened to be here.' She was, too. If poor Colonel Bartram *had* to be ill, it had happened at the best possible moment.

Sara came out of the office, Eliot following her more slowly. Sara said, 'Dr French was in, but his car went wrong this afternoon, and he hasn't managed to get a substitute yet. He'll be glad to come, but I'll have to drive over to Poltegan to get him.'

'*I'll* drive over to Poltegan,' Eliot said in a quiet voice. 'Where is it? I don't seem to know it.'

Sara glanced at him and then away again. 'You'd never find your way there in the dark. It's an awkward place to get to, if you don't know it.'

'Then I'm afraid you'll have to come with me to show me where it is,' Eliot said. 'Go and get a coat, it's chilly out, and I'll be starting my car up.'

Before Sara had time to demur he had gone out through the front door. Sara stood quite still for a moment, looking rather blankly at her sister. For a moment Averil thought she would say, '*You* go with him,' for she knew the way to Poltegan just as well as Sara did. But finally Sara gave a funny little shrug and went to get her coat.

Miss Stevens said firmly, 'I like that young man.'

Averil smiled, and the idea came to her that they might be thinking along similar lines. 'So do I ,' she said. 'Eliot's a poppet.'

They exchanged a look of mutual understanding and then Miss Stevens went back into the lounge, while Averil went upstairs and tapped on the door of the Bartrams' room. It opened a crack and Mrs Bartram's face appeared, pale and strained.

'I came to tell you that my sister's gone to fetch the doctor. They shouldn't be long. How is your husband now?'

Mrs Bartram came out on to the landing. 'Not any

better, I'm afraid. He's very hot and uncomfortable.' She spoke with the steady calmness of the soldier's wife, long accustomed to emergencies. 'Everyone is being most kind.'

Averil put a hand on her arm. 'It's rotten luck, but we'll do anything we can, you know, anything at all. Just ask for what you need. Right now I'm going down to make you a good strong cup of tea.'

In the kitchen, Joan, who was relishing the drama, left the washing up to make tea. Averil took a cup up to Mrs Bartram and stayed with her, just outside the open bedroom door, while she drank, it and talked a little, about that other time, out in Hong Kong, when her husband had been so ill.

'I wish I could remember what they called it at the hospital.' She wrinkled her brow. 'I've been trying and trying, but the name just won't come.'

'Never mind,' Averil encouraged her, 'I'm sure the doctor will be here soon and he'll be able to help. Ah, I think I hear them now.'

But when she reached the bottom of the stairs it wasn't Sara with the doctor. Bill Randall stood there, and by his side was a tall girl with pale gold hair, wearing a honey beige suede coat that must have cost the earth, and looking up at Bill in a way that would have proclaimed to the dimmest intelligence that they were on the easiest and closest terms with each other.

Averil wasn't dim, and she registered that much with a quick rush of feeling which she hadn't time to recognise before Bill said, 'Hullo, Averil, is your sister anywhere about? I'm afraid I've brought a late guest for her. I tried to warn her by phone, but I couldn't get through.'

Averil stared at the two of them in dismay. Sara would hate this happening; she always felt it her duty to be on the premises to welcome any new guest, expected or unexpected. And especially would this be so for a guest brought by Bill Randall!

But there was nothing to be done about it. 'I'm afraid my sister has had to go out,' she said, and explained the circumstances briefly.

Bill's expression was immediately serious. 'I'm sorry to hear about that. Colonel Bartram's such a nice old boy. Perhaps I'd better run you back to the north coast, Louella, if there's a crisis on here. By the way, this is Averil North, Mrs Tyndall's sister. Averil, Louella Andrews, who is by way of being one of the firm too.'

Averil smiled politely and held out her hand and the fair girl touched it momentarily and looked back to Bill. 'Oh *no*, darling, *don't* ask me to do any more driving tonight. Surely they can find me a bed here? You said the place was nearly empty, so there must be rooms vacant. Isn't there a housekeeper or something?'

' My sister does the housekeeping herself,' Averil said coolly. She recognised Louella Andrews' type. She had encountered it often in the course of selling her jewellery to the stores: buyers, heads of departments, career women one and all, superbly groomed and dressed, with soft cultivated voices. They melted to honey when they thought you had come to buy something and froze to ice when they found you wanted to sell.

But she had to be polite to this one for Sara's sake. ' My sister shouldn't be more than a few minutes, and then she'll fix you up with a room, I'm sure. Won't you have a drink while you're waiting?'

Louella Andrews brightened. 'Now that *is* a good idea.' She put a hand lightly on Bill's arm. 'Lead me to the bar, William, and you can buy me a lovely big brandy.'

Bill looked faintly amused and Averil said, ' There isn't a bar, but we can serve you with drinks in the lounge.'

' No bar?' Miss Andrews' perfect eyebrows rose. She looked over her shoulder into the lounge, where Miss Stevens sat with her book, her knitting on the arm of her chair. ' What *is* this place, Bill? An old folks' home? I see why the Old Bird sent you down to look it over.'

Averil's temper began to bubble gently. A few more remarks like that and she wouldn't be responsible for what she said. She was thankful Sara hadn't been here to hear it.

Bill took Miss Andrews firmly by the arm of her beautiful suede coat. ' Come on, we'll have our drinks in the dining room if you don't fancy the lounge. That O.K. with you, Averil?'

' Certainly,' said Averil sweetly. ' Unless you'd care to use my sister's private sitting room. I'm sure she would be delighted to put it at your disposal as you are members of the company that owns the hotel.'

Bill did look at her then, but she met his glance innocently. ' The dining room will do,' he said rather shortly, and propelled Louella in that direction.

Averil went to the kitchen and sent Joan to take their orders for drinks. Then she returned to the hall to wait for Sara and Eliot to bring the doctor back with them. She prowled about restlessly, trying not to think that Bill Randall was in the dining room drinking brandy with a horrible young woman who called him ' darling ' and looked at him as if she owned him. Perhaps she did, and good luck to her. She was no doubt the kind of girl he was used to. She, Averil

North, was not his kind of girl at all, she saw that now. She had been amusing to fill in an idle afternoon for him, and that was about it.

Her cheeks burned as she remembered how he had said, 'You're not the settling down type, are you, Averil?' No doubt he had wanted to be sure she wouldn't hang on embarrassingly when he had finished amusing himself. A delectable morsel, he had called her, when he kissed her. She couldn't remember the episode very clearly, but she was fairly sure she had shown him that she had enjoyed his kisses. She clenched her finger nails into the palms of her hands and seethed with anger—against Bill, against that beastly girl he had in the dining room with him, but most of all against herself for being so—so cheap and compliant.

Then the front door opened to admit Sara and Dr French, with Eliot behind them, and she remembered poor Colonel Bartram and his worried little wife.

Sara took the doctor straight upstairs. Eliot came over to Averil and said, 'The doctor's hired car was delivered just as we got there, so our journey wasn't really necessary. He'll drive himself back, but I think I'll hang on for a bit if you don't mind, just to see how things go, and if I can be of any help.'

Averil thought he looked tired. She said, 'Would you like something to drink? I'm sure Sara would suggest it if she were here.'

He shook his head. 'No, thanks, unless there's some coffee left.'

'I expect there is. Come into the kitchen and we'll scrounge. There's only Joan there; the formidable Mrs Bulteel has finished for the night and gone home.'

But Eliot hung back. 'How would Sara feel about my making myself at home in the kitchen?'

'Why on earth shouldn't you? You're an old family friend.' He and Sara, they were a couple of sensitives. It was going to be quite a job, getting them together again.

In the kitchen, Joan was delighted to see them. It was turning out quite an evening, what with poor Colonel Bartram, and then Mr Randall bringing that snooty, dressed-up girl back with him, and now this nice Mr Dunn sitting on the kitchen table, as easy as you please, drinking coffee and asking how she liked working here.

Presently Sara came in and Eliot slid off the table and went towards her. 'Well, what does the doctor say?'

'Dr French has just gone.' She spoke to the room in general, and the little worry lines were deep grooves between her eyebrows. 'He's given the Colonel something to reduce the temperature and he's coming in again first thing in the morning. It seems likely that he'll want to have him in hospital.'

Eliot stood looking down at her and he was frowning too. 'You look weary, Sara. Is there anything I can do to help?'

She straightened her back and gave him a polite little smile which seemed to put him at a great distance. 'Thanks, but we can manage. And thank you for running me over to the doctor's. It was very kind of you.'

Averil saw the hurt look that came into Eliot's face and she could have given Sara a good shaking. Instead she said, 'I'm afraid I've got some more bad news for you. Mr Randall has come back and brought a guest with him, a Miss Andrews. I gather she's in the company too. They're in the dining room now, having drinks. I wasn't sure what to do with her and I didn't want to go and knock Mrs Bulteel up.' The Bulteels lived in a cottage in the village.

Sara said grimly, ' It just needed that. One doesn't reckon on casual guests at this time of night, in this kind of hotel. Surely they could have rung up and warned us?'

' Mr Randall said he tried, but the number was engaged. It must have been when you were ringing the doctor. Is there a room ready, or—'

Sara nodded wearily. ' Oh yes, there's a room ready, except for making up the bed. I'll go and see to that now.'

Joan stepped forward sturdily. ' I'll come an' help 'ee, Mrs Tyndall. I'm in no hurry to get home tonight.'

Sara gave her the kind of look she should have given Eliot earlier—grateful, affectionate. ' Thanks, Joan. We'll have sheets from the airing room, not the ones in the linen cupboard.'

She hurried to the door, passing Eliot on the way. She paused briefly, her eyes meeting his and then sliding away again quickly. ' Goodnight, Eliot.' She followed Joan up the back stairs.

Eliot stood quite still, looking as if he had been slapped. Then he walked slowly back to the table and put down his cup. ' Well, that seems to be that. I'd better make myself scarce.'

Averil exploded into indignation. ' *Well!* If she wasn't my own sister, I'd—'

He shook his head at her, smiling very wryly. ' Don't blame Sara. She can't forgive me for what happened years ago, that's all it is.'

' *She* can't forgive *you*? You've got it the wrong way round, haven't you? Surely the forgiving ought to be on your side.'

' Oh no, it doesn't work that way. You always have

a lurking grudge against someone you think you've treated badly, that's life.'

She suddenly felt very young and out of her depth. ' Is it? Then I don't think much of it.'

She walked with Eliot to his car. Outside, the breeze was fresh and cool against her cheeks, and when she looked up the stars were thick and brilliant in the black velvet sky. She drew in a long breath. 'That helps to put things into proportion, doesn't it?'

She heard Eliot chuckle as he climbed into his car and switched on the lights. Then he leaned out and patted her arm. 'Don't worry, Averil. I'll be back to have another try.'

She stood and watched him drive away, full of relief at those last words. Eliot was a darling and she could only hope that Sara would realise it in time.

When the sound of the engine had died away to a purr in the distance she still stood there. What she really wanted to do was to creep up to bed. But if she stayed outside a little longer she might avoid seeing Bill Randall and the Andrews woman again tonight.

Suddenly the telephone rang in the hall. She checked her first impulse to go in and answer it. It might well be Kevin ringing her, and there had been enough to cope with this evening without having to argue with Kevin about when she was going back to Exeter. So she turned and walked quickly down the drive and out into the lane.

There was no moon yet, but the stars were so bright that they threw a pale glow over everything—the high hedges, the roadway rough with loose stones, the lushly growing verges where later the slender mullein would send up its tall yellow spikes.

She reached Methuselah's field. He was standing patiently by the gate, as usual, his head resting on the bar. She stroked his nose and murmured, 'Don't you ever go to sleep, you funny old donkey? Or do you stay awake and dream about seeing the world, like *he* said?'

There she was again, thinking about Bill Randall, and it simply wouldn't do. With an effort she turned her thoughts to her work and the studio. She really shouldn't be away too long, for she had plenty of commissions to keep her busy. The studio was beginning to justify its existence and the time and money she had spent on it. She had several rings and a necklace in various stages of construction, and there was one special job—an opal brooch—which promised to be fascinating. It was for a twenty-first birthday present, and no expense to be spared. She tried to visualise the design of delicate gold tendrils she had worked out tentatively. These were the things which had so satisfactorily filled her life up to a few days ago. So it was all the more maddening to find that her mind should skitter rapidly back to Bill Randall and the girl he had brought to the hotel with him. It was time, she decided, to take herself seriously in hand. Just because he had taken her out once; just because he had kissed her—and the kiss had got a bit out of hand—it didn't mean that she had any claim on him. There were no doubt dozens of girls in his life, past, present, and future, especially as he was (as he had so carefully told her) averse to 'settling down.'

No, there was no reason at all to feel vaguely let down. Still, it was a pity that he had found it necessary to give her a wrong impression—deliberately, no doubt. All that thing about having to go up to the north coast on business! It would have been so easy, and much more honest, to say that he had another date, and of course she wouldn't have minded. Or would she?

She banged her fists on the gate. Oh, Methuselah, I think I'm a bigger donkey than you are! I must be getting feeble-minded to care what a man like Bill Randall does or says. Any sane girl wouldn't give him a second thought—except for an amusing afternoon. Keep the thing in perspective, Averil, can't you?

Then she saw a tall, shadowy figure approaching her down the lane and her resolution dissolved in this rather frightening reaction to his physical presence. Her heart thumped and her mouth went dry.

'Hullo, I thought I might find you saying goodnight to Methuselah, the lucky donkey.' She couldn't see his face, but she could picture the way his eyes squeezed up when he smiled. 'Your sister was looking for you, to take a phone call. Someone called Kevin. Sorry, I couldn't help overhearing.'

'It doesn't matter,' she said, in sudden confusion.

'What doesn't matter? That you missed your call, or that I heard a private conversation?'

'It couldn't have been very private. Sara's only met him once. They wouldn't have anything private to say to each other.'

He chuckled. 'That's a matter of opinion.'

'You're talking in riddles,' she said crossly.

'Am I?' He leaned his back against the gate beside her, much too close for her peace of mind, but it would be gauche to move away, and no doubt would give him another opportunity to be amused at her expense. 'Well, let's skip Kevin for the moment. I wanted to see you before you turned in.'

'Did you? I can't imagine why.' She meant to sound coolly unconcerned, but it came out horribly pert and flippant.

'I wanted to apologise for Louella's disgusting display of bad manners a few minutes ago. After our talk this afternoon I know how you and your sister feel about the Cormorant, and what Louella said must have been hurtful. I'm sure she didn't mean to be so destructively critical. You see, she's recently been appointed the Old Bird's private assistant and I think it's gone to her head somewhat. She's making very heavy weather of being a woman in a man's world and all that sort of thing. Seems to think it's necessary to be brusque and tough. She'll grow out of it, she's not really tough.' He chuckled tolerantly. Or was it affectionately? 'She's quite a gal, our Louella.'

'I'm sure she is,' Averil said politely. 'And there's really no need to apologise for Miss Andrews. She was perfectly entitled to say whatever she thought.'

With what she hoped was dignity she began to walk back up the lane, but one strong hand shot out and took hold of her arm. 'Hey, what's all this?' There was laughter in his voice. 'I thought we were pals.'

The closeness of his body and the pressure of his fingers gripping her wrist completely bereft her of speech.

'Also,' he went on, 'I want to give you your little bit of kitsch. Promise you won't run away if I let you go?'

Silence.

'Promise,' he insisted, giving her wrist a little shake.

'All right,' she murmured.

He released her and fumbled in his pocket for the little brooch made of yellow shells. 'My privilege to pin it on?' he said softly, and without waiting for a reply he bent down and pinned it to her dress. His dark hair almost brushed her cheek; it smelled clean and faintly spicy. It was all she could do not to lay her face against it.

'There!' he said at last. 'A present for a good girl. You know what,' he added, and there was surprise as well as amusement in his voice, 'I really believe you are.'

She was much too confused not to fall straight into the trap. 'I am what?' she said.

He laughed aloud. 'A good girl, of course.' Suddenly he bent down and touched her forehead lightly with his lips. Then he turned her round by the shoulders and gave her a little push towards the hotel.

'Go on,' he said, 'run. Or I won't be responsible for the consequences. Go and ring the boy-friend and put him out of his misery.'

Averil hesitated for just one second. Then she ran.

CHAPTER V

When Averil got up to the bedroom she found Sara sitting up in bed, creaming her face, her dark hair falling softly on to her shoulders.

She said, 'I thought I'd turn in while I got the chance. I must be on the job early in the morning.'

Averil came and sat on the edge of the bed. 'How's the Colonel now?'

'Sleeping, but rather restless, his wife says. I've told her to come and rouse me in the night if I can be of any help.' She took a tissue from a packet beside the bed. 'I've been looking for you. Kevin was asking for you on the phone, but I couldn't find you anywhere.'

'I went out for a breath of air before I came up to bed. I walked down the lane a little way.'

Sara said quickly, 'With the Randall man? I saw him go out.'

Averil got up and went over to the dressing table. 'No, not with "the Randall man". We met later. By accident,' she added.

Sara finished removing the cream from her face before she spoke again. Then she said, 'All right, love, I get the message and I'm a cranky, interfering elder sister.'

'Rubbish!' Averil spun round. 'Of course you're not, and I didn't intend to suggest it. It's just that —it's not like you to be unfair, Sal. You don't really know anything about Bill Randall, do you, except that he's come here from Ravens. You don't even know why.'

'Do *you* know? Did he tell you this afternoon? If he did say anything, Averil, please tell me. I'd much rather know the truth than have to go on guessing and imagining things.'

'No, he didn't tell me. We didn't talk business. But I *did* talk a bit about the Cormorant and I told him how we'd both looked on it as home for ages and ages, and how attached we were to it.' She walked slowly back to the bed and stood looking down at her sister's worried face. 'He seemed to understand, Sal, really he did. He wasn't just putting on an act. He said he'd do his very best to see that your interests were protected. That was fair enough, surely?'

But she knew from Sara's sigh and the little shake of her head that she wasn't convinced, so she changed the subject. 'What did Kevin want? Did he say?' She began to get undressed.

'He didn't say anything to me. It was you he wanted to talk to. He seemed disappointed when I couldn't find you.' There was a small silence. 'He asked if you were—all right, and I said you were, and that was about the limit of our conversation. He seems a very nice man, Averil.   Sincere.'

'Sincere?   Yes, I suppose he is.'   Averil sat down and peeled off her tights.   She knew that Sara wanted to hear about Kevin—how serious it was between the two of them—but she didn't want to talk about it.   It was incredible that it was only yesterday morning that she had said goodbye to him; it seemed like years. She had to make quite an effort to remember how he looked, standing outside his boutique with the sun glinting on his large important glasses and his crinkly fair hair.   She said idly, ' He wants to manage me, Sal, and I don't take kindly to being managed, as I think you know.'

She smiled very ruefully at Sara, and suddenly the warmth and sympathy flowed between them again. Sara laughed.   ' Don't I just?   You always were an independent little cuss.   Remember that white rabbit?'

Somebody had given Averil a cuddly toy rabbit, when she was about four.   It had long, silky white fur, pink glass eyes, and a button of a nose that seemed to twitch.   Averil adored it, carried it everywhere, took it to bed with her, shared her sweets with it.   The rabbit was, for days, quite the most important and beloved thing in her life.   Then, one terrible day, Sara discovered that the pink glass eyes and soft furry legs were all held on to the body by long, dangerous pins.   Sara, at fourteen, took her position as elder sister very seriously indeed.   Suitably shocked and outraged, she had taken the rabbit away, and Averil had been desolate.   She had wept and raged and pleaded in vain. Then, a few days later, Sara had found her little sister playing happily with the remains of the rabbit, which she must have unearthed in a kitchen drawer.   The toy, bereft of its lethal pins, was in several pieces, but that didn't seem to matter to Averil.

'I *like* him that way,' she had insisted to Sara, who had suggested trying to sew the rabbit together. 'I like him *my* way.'

Sara laughed again now, remembering. 'Yes, you always liked to do things your own way. But perhaps Kevin only wants to do things the best way for you.'

'Perhaps,' Averil said. 'I don't know him well enough to be sure. We'll have to wait and see, won't we?' Her voice was remote, hardly interested.

Sara leaned forward and said, 'If I seem interfering it's only because I don't want to see you make the same mess of your life that I made, love. You do know that, don't you?'

Averil came quickly across the room, her brief nightie swishing round her legs, and enclosed her sister in a warm hug. 'Yes, of course I do.'

'And about Mr Randall—'

'Yes?' Averil was suddenly quiet.

'I think it's because he—' Sara continued the sentence with difficulty '—because he's so like Roy. As soon as I saw him I saw the likeness. Not only his looks, but his manner, his outlook, everything about him.'

This explained a lot of things. Averil stood up and walked over to the window, looking out into the cool darkness. Then she turned round and said gently but very firmly, 'I'm a big girl now, Sal. I take my own risks and accept the consequences. And I don't think he's really very like Roy.'

Sara said bleakly, 'I don't think you can remember what Roy was like. You were only thirteen or fourteen, weren't you?' But Averil did remember, and she was sure Sara was wrong. Bill was nothing like Roy, really. There was something strong beneath Bill's foolery, she was sure there was. And there had been nothing strong about Roy. There couldn't have been, could there, or he wouldn't have acted the way he did.

She looked at Sara's unhappy face and she wanted to comfort her, to tell her that she hadn't made a mess of her life; that it was absurd to be resigned to that idea at her age. She wanted to speak to her about Eliot. But of course she couldn't, for why should she expect Sara to take her advice, any more than she was prepared to accept Sara's? They both had to work things out for themselves.

So she said goodnight to Sara, switched off the light and got into her little camp bed. She made herself think about Kevin, as she lay awake in the dark. Ever since she bought the Mini and decided to come away his attitude had seemed to change, to become much more possessive. She wondered for the first time if he had marriage in mind, and what she would say if he asked her. She had never considered marriage seriously, although there had been plenty of men friends in the background of her life, one or two of whom had wanted to move into the foreground. But she had always held back, telling herself that she must first of all prove that she was capable of making a success of her art work. That had been her excuse, but now she faced the fact that it had really been because no man had ever had the power to arouse and disturb her until her senses swam. Not until now. Not until Bill Randall.

She had hung her dress on the chair beside her bed and now her hand went out and groped for the yellow shell brooch. Under the bedclothes her fingers traced the outline of the shells which had spent the afternoon in his pocket, warm against his body. It was madness, feeling like this, and she must stop it. But not yet, not tonight. She snuggled down under the bedclothes, holding the little brooch close in her hand, and was asleep almost immediately.

Next morning the Colonel was worse. 'They're sending an ambulance out from the hospital at Truro,' Sara told Averil, after the doctor had been and gone.

The two girls were having a scrappy breakfast at the end of the kitchen table—Sara because she hadn't time for anything else, and Averil because she didn't want to go into the dining room and meet Bill Randall with the Andrews woman.

'Is there any way I could help, do you think?' she asked Sara. 'The Mini might be of some use to Mrs Bartram, by way of transport.'

'Could be,' said Sara. 'Why don't you go up and ask? I think Mrs Bartram would be glad of your company until the ambulance arrives, anyway.'

So Averil gulped down the remainder of her coffee and ran upstairs, to tap gently on the door of the Bartrams' room.

The curtains were drawn against the strong morning light, and Mrs Bartram was packing a case with the Colonel's things. She smiled tremulously at Averil and seemed glad to see her. 'He's sleeping again now,' she whispered with a glance towards the bed. 'The doctor gave him an injection. He's been terribly restless for the last couple of hours.'

In the dimness, Mrs Bartram's face was very white and her eyes puffy. 'Have you had any sleep?' Averil asked, but she could guess the anwer before she asked.

'Me? Oh yes, I dozed off now and then.' Her thin little hands fluttered above the open case. 'Do you imagine he'll need his electric shaver? I really don't know how they manage these things in England. Do you know, I can't ever remember Hugh being in hospital in his own country—isn't it odd?' Her laugh was a high nervous sound. 'Often out in the East, of course—and then that last awful time in Ireland.' She sighed. 'I'd thought we'd finished with all that now that Hugh has retired, but—oh well, I mustn't moan, must I? That won't do any good at all. Now, my dear, if you'd pass me that little pile of handkerchiefs out of the top drawer—thank you, you're being so kind to me, you and your sister too. I really am most grateful to you both.'

Averil said, 'I was wondering if I could be any use to you for transport? I've got my own little car here, and I could come along to the hospital, perhaps, and then take you anywhere you wanted, after you've got the Colonel settled in. Unless you're driving yourself, of course.'

'Oh no, I don't drive—I've never really wanted to. And anyway, I should go with Hugh in the ambulance.' She looked at Averil uncertainly. 'It really is most kind of you, but I don't think you should give up your holiday time like this.'

'I'd like to come with you—if you'd like to have me.'

'Oh, my dear, I would, very much.' For the first time Mrs Bartram's voice was choky with tears.

Averil said briskly, 'That's fine, then. I'll go down and tell Sara what we've arranged. Then I'll follow on after the ambulance, and sort of hover in the background so I'll be there when you want me.' She went to the window and peeped round the curtains. 'Yes, they're here now.'

The ambulance crew were as quick, efficient, and cheery as ambulance crews always are, and very soon the Colonel, swathed in blankets on his stretcher, was comfortably installed. Mrs Bartram climbed in beside him and Sara handed in the case, while Averil started the Mini's engine.

The ambulance crunched over the gravel of the drive and Averil put the Mini in gear carefully. She leaned out of the window and said to Sara, 'Expect me when you see me, Sal.' Then she let in the clutch and followed the ambulance along the drive and round the corner.

The steep lane to the village was narrow, and the ambulance was wide. Half way up it had to slow almost to a stop to pass a car coming down. Averil drew in to the left and changed down into second. Then she recognised the passing car as it drew alongside and her heart gave a familiar jump; her foot slipped off the accelerator, and the engine stalled.

Desperately she pulled on the hand-brake as the other car stopped and Bill Randall wound down the window. 'Where are you off to, so early in the morning?'

She explained briefly and he nodded and said in his serious voice, 'That's a kind act. Can you manage? Would you like me to come along? I'm driving Louella back up north, but she could very well wait.'

She started the engine again, hoping he wouldn't notice that it had stopped. 'Oh no, thank you very much. I don't really know how long we shall be, or what's going to happen.' She grinned briefly. 'I'll drive carefully and I won't do anything silly.'

He didn't smile. 'Mind you don't,' he said, and drew his car ahead to let her pass.

Starting the car on a hill as steep as this was something she hadn't yet tackled, but mercifully she managed it quite neatly. The ambulance was out of sight, but she caught up with it just beyond the village. She fell into position behind, and all the way to Truro she concentrated hard on her driving.

But some small part at the back of her mind was busy with Bill Randall. It seemed that whatever she was doing she couldn't quite get him out of her thoughts for long. Had he really meant it, she wondered, when he offered to come along with her? She didn't suppose so; Louella was not the kind of girl who would take kindly to being kept waiting, and Louella seemed to hold a very high-up position in the company. Evidently one of Bill's assignments was to drive Louella about, and no doubt he enjoyed it. She remembered the amused, affectionate note in his voice as he said, 'She's quite a girl, our Louella.' Remembered, too, the way Louella had let her hand linger on his arm; the way her eyes had gone slowly and almost insolently to his as she called him 'darling'. Impatiently Averil brought her attention back to her driving. This wouldn't do at all; the man was beginning to claim all her attention, which was absurd when she had only known him a couple of days. A little teasing; an afternoon out; a kiss at the end of it. What did it add up to? Nothing at all in his book, she guessed. But in hers?

Nothing in mine either, she said firmly, aloud, and fixed her eyes on the back of the ambulance in front.

When Averil finally got back to the hotel, her mission partly accomplished, it was almost lunch time. Sara was in the hall, talking to Miss Stevens, and they both pounced on her with questions.

'It all went very smoothly,' she told them. 'Mrs Bartram seemed pleased and reassured with the way everything was managed at the hospital. She saw the resident doctor, and later on she will probably be able to see the specialist who is taking charge of the case.

She's decided to stay in Truro, for the time being, so that she can be near the hospital, and I managed to get a room for her at that little private hotel near the Cathedral—you know the place I mean, Sara?'

' The Close?'

' Yes, that's the one. It's nice and quiet and homely there and I think she'll be comfy. I've promised to collect a few things from her room and take them over there this evening, then I can see her and find out how things are going. I think I'd better go up and pack her case now, while I remember what she needs.'

She smiled at them and went towards the stairs. Before she reached the top she heard Miss Stevens' clear, headmistressy voice say warmly, ' That's a good girl you've got there, Mrs Tyndall.'

Averil grinned to herself. A good girl! That was what Bill had called her. Only he hadn't meant it in quite the same way.

She had lunch with Miss Stevens and they were the only occupants of the dining room. Afterwards Miss Stevens went upstairs for her rest, grumbling a little at the necessity. Sara seemed busy in the office, so Averil decided to go down to the sea. So far this visit she had only seen it from the top of the cliff, and she had a longing to walk along at the edge of the tide, to sniff the seaweed and listen to the hiss and crash as the waves broke over the rocks.

The sun was still shining but a fresh breeze had sprung up, so she tied a scarf over her hair and set out. She had collected some sugar lumps for Methuselah, but when she reached the field she saw that he was otherwise engaged with the children from the village. Sara allowed them to come down and play with him, on the understanding that they were careful to close the gate, and that there was always one of the older children there to be responsible for the little ones.

This time it was Tim Ellis, the eldest boy of Rob Ellis from the Ship, and he had two of his small brothers with him. Averil paused at the gate and called, ' Hullo, Tim. What are you doing, away from school?'

He gave her his wide, gap-toothed grin. ' Me mum's had to go to have her eyes tested, so I'm staying back to look after them.' He jerked a thumb towards the two little ones, who were clamouring to be the first to be lifted up on to Methuselah's back.

Averil stayed and watched them for a while and she could almost believe that Methuselah was enjoying the proceedings as much as the children, as he plodded along patiently with the smallest redhead on his back, hanging on with shrieks of glee to the old donkey's thick grey mane. Perhaps he was remembering the old days when he had a useful job of work to do and didn't just stand about in a field all day long.

' Be careful to lock the gate,' she called to Tim, and she waved to them and went on down to the sea.

The tide was low, and still going out. Averil pulled off her sandals, rolled up her trousers, and ran down over the wet sand to the edge of the sea. After the first shivering shock the Atlantic chill of the water was exciting and she waded along the edge of the tide, letting the small waves lap over her ankles, while the wind teased tendrils of hair from beneath her scarf and slapped it against her cheeks. Oh, it was glorious here! She threw back her head and laughed with the joy of being young and alive and healthy.

But enough was enough, and the water really was icy. Soon she made her way back to the shelter of the high cliffs behind the cove, and sat on a rock to rub the sand from between her toes and wait for the breeze to dry them.

Then she looked up and saw Bill Randall, and the sudden surprise of seeing him coming towards her in the sunshine seemed to complete her uprush of heady joy. He was wearing chocolate brown slacks and a sand-coloured roll-neck sweater today, and he really did look gorgeous, she admitted with a little catch of her breath. Any girl would go overboard for him, no doubt of that. She just had to be careful *she* didn't. She was a girl with a career of her own, and mooning about with a broken heart over a man who had taken great care to explain that he ' wasn't the settling down type ' had no place in her life.

' Hi! ' He raised a hand in greeting as he came up to her, and lowered himself to the rock at her side. ' How did you manage this morning? '

She told him just what she had told Sara and Miss Stevens and he listened gravely. When she had finished he nodded and said, ' I hope the Colonel comes through. They seem such a—what's the old word?—such a devoted couple. It's hard for one to be left alone.' He was silent for a moment, looking out at the wide expanse of sea with the tossing, foam-flecked white tips to the waves. ' That's what happened to the Old Bird, you know.'

' Mr Raven? '

' Yes. He and my grandmother had such plans for retiring. Then she died, suddenly and unexpectedly. That was when he threw himself into this hotel thing —it gave him something to hold on to.'

' Mr Raven is your grandfather? ' Now that she knew, it all seemed to fit into place; it explained such a lot of things: why he was an apparently top member of the firm and yet had told Sara that he was learning the business from the bottom up; why he was driving

Mr Raven's expensive car; his attitude to Louella Andrews. Oh, everything, really!

'Yes, didn't you know? I thought your sister would have told you.'

'I'm sure she would have done—if she'd known.'

He turned and looked at her in surprise. 'There's evidently been a hitch in communications somewhere. Not that it really matters—I don't rate any special privileges. I'm a very minor member of the firm as yet.'

She smiled. 'But being groomed for stardom?' To step into the shoes of a millionaire grandfather—that put him right outside her world, which, in an odd way, was a relief. At least now she knew for certain that letting herself dream about him was definitely *out*.

He replied very wryly, 'I suppose you might call it that. It all depends what you think of as being most worth while.'

'But surely—you'll take over Ravens when your grandfather retires?'

He nodded sombrely. 'That's what I promised, and that's what I'll try to do, if it kills me.'

He drew up his legs and hugged his knees and there was a long silence. Then he said suddenly, 'The clock struck midnight, you see, and the ball was over.' He was making a joke of it, but she knew it wasn't a joke —whatever it was.

She was wondering how she could frame a question that wouldn't seem to be too inquisitive when he turned to her with a grin and added, 'I'm talking in riddles, and that's a bad habit . What actually happened was that when I came down from Cambridge the Old Bird naturally wanted me to come into the business with him. I wanted to go along with him, in one way, because I owe him a good deal—he and my grandmother took me over when both my parents were killed in one of the V 2 raids over London at the end of the war. But I also had an insatiable yearning to get out and about in the world, on my own. Eventually we reached a compromise. I was to be an absolutely free agent and do anything I wanted to until such time as the Old Bird felt he was reaching retiring age. Then I should come back, in plenty of time to learn the ins and out of the hotel business before he gave up. I mustn't grumble—I've had nine glorious years and I've been to most places and done most things I wanted, and now the time's come to turn myself into a serious and respectable citizen.'

'But the idea doesn't fill you with joy?'

'Does it show so much?'

Averil smiled. 'If I were your grandfather I shouldn't be too hopeful of the "serious" bit. You don't take much seriously, do you?'

He sighed heavily. 'I suppose you're right. I have an idea that's why the Old Bird sent Louella down to these parts—as bait.'

'Bait?'

He laughed aloud at her expression. 'Lure, if you prefer the word. He wants me to settle down, and he thinks it's more likely to happen if I get myself a wife —preferably one who's clever as well as beautiful and will help me to run the business when the time comes. Louella seems to fill the bill on both counts. She's intelligent as well as beautiful.'

There was a silence.

'Isn't she?' he insisted with a wicked glance towards her.

'Yes. Oh yes, of course. I was only wondering—'

'Wondering what?' he asked softly.

'No, it's not my business. Merely idle curiosity.'

He burst out laughing at that. 'A girl in a million —one who can resist asking personal questions, even though she's dying to know the answer.'

Her eyes sparkled. 'I am *not* dying to know the answer!'

'Just as well,' he said mildly, 'because I don't know it myself yet.' He twisted his legs round on the rock and faced her earnestly. 'Now, tell me. Give me some good advice. Do *you* think I ought to settle down?'

He was fooling, of course, but she chose to take the question seriously. 'Everyone has to settle down some time,' she said. 'It's nice to play around for a while, but you have to have an aim in life.' She laughed wryly. 'Oh dear, that sounds pompous.'

'Not a bit of it. It sounds like common sense. What's your aim in life, Averil?'

'My work, I suppose,' she said, because it always had been. 'That sounds pretty pompous too, but it isn't really. I don't consider myself an artist; I just like messing about in a studio, making things.' She wished it didn't sound so feeble. She wished, just for a moment, that she was intelligent and sophisticated, like Louella Andrews, and capable of holding down a top job.

She expected him to laugh at her, but he didn't. He stared out at the horizon for quite a long time before he spoke again. Then he said, 'Thanks, Averil, you've done me a good turn. You've helped me to make up my mind about something.'

About Louella Andrews? She waited, but when he didn't seem to be going to add to the statement she got up and jumped down from the rock. 'It's cold, I'm going in.' She shivered, turning to look up to where the sun had been shining a few minutes ago.

Then she froze. Bill was beside her and she spun round, clutching his arm. 'Look up there, for heaven's sake!'

Far above them on the very edge of the cliff, silhouetted against the sky, stood Methuselah.

'Those wretched children, they must have left the gate open!' wailed Averil, starting to run towards the long, steep flight of steps that climbed up the side of the cliff. Getting the old donkey back into his field might be a major operation. Once before, when he had strayed, it had taken Sara and her more than an hour, pleading and pulling and pushing, before they finally got him back. Methuselah was true to his donkey clan—as stubborn as they came when it suited him.

She reached the top of the steps, panting, with Bill close behind, and looked for Methuselah, but he was no longer where she had seen him.

'He's gone.' She felt icy cold, suddenly. 'Oh, Bill, where has he gone, do you think?'

He said calmly, 'We'd better go and take a look. Which way do you imagine a donkey out for a stroll would choose?'

He was making a joke of it, but she knew that he was thinking, as she was, of the cliff edge and the sheer drop to the jagged rocks far below. She groped for the safety rail at the top of the steps and held on.

Bill gripped her arm harder. 'He wouldn't, you know. Animals are incredibly canny about where they put their feet down. Come on, let's look.'

The cliff top here was rough and irregular, with small rises and hollows, and matted with thorn bushes and clumps of tall, straggly grasses. There was hardly enough cover for a large dog, let alone a donkey, but they searched from end to end of the promontory.

Finally Averil set her teeth and made for the edge of the cliff, but Bill pulled her away. 'Better let me. I've a wonderful head for heights.' He walked to the edge and looked over.

She held her breath and waited. When he turned round again he said slowly, 'Yes, he's down there, all right.' She felt all the blood go out of her head as he gripped her arm tight and gave her a little shake and said, 'No. *No*, Averil. He hasn't fallen, he's quite safe. He's on a sort of ledge, about twenty feet down.'

She let out her breath on a long sigh of relief. 'Tell me,' he said, 'before, when he used to give donkey rides on the sands—where was it? Not here, surely?'

She knew that he was giving her time to pull herself together and she was grateful. 'No,' she said shakily, 'on the other side of the headland, where the holiday crowds go. Not many people come to this cove. You can't take very small children down all those steps.'

He nodded. 'How do you get down to the beach there?'

'Oh, it's much easier. The donkey man used to lead them down a sort of wide slipway by the cliff, just a gentle slope.'

'Yes, well, I'd say Methuselah has a sort of memory, then. The ledge he's on starts quite wide at the top and then gets narrower and narrower, until it goes to nothing. That's the point he's reached.'

'Let me look.'

He took her hand and held it firmly. 'Steady now.'

She leaned forward and peered over the edge. It was just as he had said. Methuselah was standing quietly and patiently, as he always stood, at the point where the narrowing shelf of rock disappeared altogether into the face of the cliff. On one side of him was the sheer wall of granite, on the other a sickening vertical drop to the jagged rocks below.

She stepped back and whispered, 'Oh, what shall we do?'

'Think,' said Bill grimly. 'And think fast. Do you know where the nearest coastguard station is?'

'At Gorran Haven. It must be—oh, eight or nine miles away.'

He considered that for a moment, then he said, 'We'll see what we can do ourselves first. Look, here are my keys. You'll find a coil of rope in the boot of my car, and I think there's a sleeping bag too. Be as quick as you can. I'll keep an eye on Methuselah, but somehow I don't think he'll do anything silly.'

Her legs were like elastic, but she managed to run, stumbling over the rough path up to the hotel and into the garage. There was nobody about and she didn't stop to look for anybody. In any case the only other man around was Bulteel, and he was elderly and not very quick on the uptake.

She found the key to unlock the boot of Bill's car and lifted the lid. Fleetingly she remembered how once she had imagined a boot full of elegant luggage, containing elegant clothes, and she could almost have laughed at what she saw was the reality. Here was an old rucksack, a stout stick, climbing boots, a coil of rope. There was a sleeping bag too, which looked as if it had seen years of service. She hoisted the rope over her shoulder, grabbed the sleeping bag, and ran back the way she had come.

'Good girl, that's the stuff.' Bill's eyes seemed to brighten at the sight of the rope; there was a sort of tense, controlled urgency about him now. He had found a tough tree, standing a little way back from the cliff edge in a hollow, one of the stunted trees bent over almost double by the winds up here. He left the main part of the coil of rope lying on the cliff, securing the middle to the tree trunk and leaving two ends free. 'This'll hold, I think.' He gave the tree a good tug. 'It seems firmly rooted.'

Averil said in a small voice, 'What are you going to do?'

He straightened up. 'We're going to persuade Methuselah to back along that ledge, the way he came —I hope. But first of all we've got to get a rope round him in case he gets awkward.' He picked up one end of the rope and was securing it to the sleeping bag, which he had first zipped open. 'I'll tell you my idea —but of course it's only improvising and it may not work. I shall climb the rock from below and come up in front of Methuselah. When I call I want you to lower both ends of the rope to me—one for me and the other for Methuselah.'

She thought of the sheer, jagged rock, of the drop, and her inside lurched. 'But you *can't*—you mustn't—' she stammered.

He held her arm and said very gently, 'Look, my dear, there's no time to show you my medals now, but you may take it I'm quite an experienced climber. Please trust me, Averil. It'll be all right.'

She bit her lip hard and looked up into his eyes. They had a steady blue glitter, like deep sea water. 'Will you trust me and do as I say?' he urged.

She nodded. 'Yes.' And then again, 'Yes, Bill.'

'Good.' He carried the rope ends, one with the sleeping bag, to a particular spot on the cliff edge, looking over several times to check the position. Then he stood back. 'Let's go, then. When I call, lower the bag gently until I tell you to stop. Lie down flat on your tummy as you do it, and pay out the rope little by little. Right?'

'Right.'

'Don't look down until you have to,' he said. 'I'll give you a shout now and then to report progress. It may take some time,' he added.

She nodded speechlessly. He stood there for a moment, then he bent down and kissed her briefly and firmly full on her mouth before he turned and made for the steps to the beach below.

Time ceased to register. She sat down near the cliff edge, but not too near, and pulled up little tufts of springy grass, building them into a kind of wreath, which turned into something like a bird's nest. Several times Bill's voice drifted up from below, distant at first but gradually sounding nearer. Then there was a long time with no sound and she went on sitting there, her fingers automatically twisting and plaiting the grass almost as if she were twisting the wire for a brooch or a pendant. The silence went on and on. She wanted to call, but suddenly fear and imagination had closed up her throat. She touched her fingers to the lips he had kissed and thought, quite clearly and definitely: If he falls and kills himself then I don't want to go on living either. It didn't seem exaggerated or melodramatic at that moment, it just seemed plain fact.

'Averil—hullo!' The sound came from quite close below her, and it had a triumphant ring about it.

'Hullo!' she answered in a flood of relief.

She looked over the edge then, lying on her tummy as he had said. 'Bill—are you all right?'

'Fine,' he called back. 'The last patch was a bit tricky, but this is as safe as an armchair.'

It didn't look to Averil like any sort of a chair, but he certainly appeared to have a handhold and his feet were firmly anchored in a low hollow ridge, like a trough. He was quite near Methuselah now and he was talking to him as man to man. She only hoped Methuselah got the drift.

'I'll have the ropes now, one by one,' Bill called up. 'The one without the bag first.' He caught the end as she lowered it and, leaning back against the rock, began to secure it round his body. She looked away quickly, fighting with a deadly sick feeling, but at last she heard his voice: 'Now the other end.' She braced herself to look over the edge again and saw that he had the rope firmly hitched round him, and she let out a long quivering sigh of relief.

Then followed the long, tricky manœuvre of roping the donkey. How Bill managed it she never knew, for she daren't look, but somehow he did. After what seemed like hours, punctuated by grunts and muttered expletives from Bill, there was a cry of triumph. She looked once more and this time saw that the sleeping bag was at least partly wrapped round Methuselah's body, with the rope looped and knotted so that he was in a sort of hammock.

'You've done it!' she exulted in a whisper that was carried away by the wind. 'Oh, Bill darling, you've done it!'

'I'm going to test out my theory now and see if it works,' he shouted up. 'If it doesn't we'll have to contact the coastguard station.'

Very slowly he eased himself from where he had been working, just above Methuselah's body, to a spot straight in front of him, on a level with his nose. Then, inch by inch, he began to move towards him. After a moment when the donkey stood his ground, ears flattened, nose lifted, he reacted as he always did when anyone approached him too close: he began to back away.

The ledge on which he was standing was so narrow that it seemed at first that he *must* slip over, but he didn't, and with every yard the ledge widened out. Averil lay on her front, staring down, hardly daring to breathe, as the curious procession went on below her, Methuselah stepping backwards, and Bill, finding handholds on the rock, keeping close in front of his nose.

'How much slack left on the ropes?' Bill shouted up presently.

'Enough,' she called back, paying it out as they moved further along the ledge. Then, all of a sudden, the danger was over; the ledge of rock widened out into a grass-covered path and rose to meet the cliff top at the place where Methuselah must have started down. A minute or two later Bill and the old donkey were standing beside her.

Bill tethered Methuselah closely to the tree and then threw himself down on the grass. 'That,' he murmured, 'was quite a party.'

Averil's knees were as weak as water and she was suddenly kneeling beside him. 'Bill, how can I thank you enough? You were absolutely wonderful!'

He grinned faintly, lying back on the grass. 'As a matter of fact, I rather enjoyed it. I hoped there might be a spot of climbing when I came down here; that's why I brought all the gear along with me. Good thing I did, as it happens.'

'Climbing—yes, perhaps, but not this.'

He pulled himself up and began to loosen the knots in the rope around his body. 'Look, my dear, let's not make a big thing out of it. It was a toss-up whether it would work, and fortunately it did, that's all. And, if you don't mind, I'd really rather you didn't spread it around.'

His eyes were fixed on the knot he was undoing, and she saw with amazement that he was embarrassed. When she didn't reply after a moment he looked up at her and added wryly, ' I hate a fuss, so if you love me—don't.'

If you love me—what a way to put it! She looked into the vivid blue eyes and thought dizzily, *You'll never know how much.* But the thing to do was to keep it light at all costs, so she smiled at him, lowering her lashes, and murmured, ' I'm not sure I love you enough to keep quiet. People ought to know what you did.'

Her heart began to hammer at what she saw in his face and she thought, I'm flirting with danger and enjoying it, just as he says he enjoyed the danger and excitement down there on the face of the rock.

He pushed the rope away. ' If you insist on making me a hero, then I claim the hero's reward,' he said, smiling, ' and I think you know what that is.' And he reached out and pulled her down on to the grass beside him.

The kiss was not gentle at all and it seemed to go on for ages. The wind swept back her hair, which some time or other had lost its restraining scarf, and the wiry grasses prickled her skin through her woollen jumper.

At last she pushed him away. ' Bill, that's enough reward. No, please—Methuselah's watching us!'

Reluctantly he let her go and they got to their feet, brushing the bits of grass and dried bracken from their clothes, laughing together like a couple of children.

It was just then that Averil looked round to see Kevin coming down the lane towards them.

CHAPTER VI

Kevin quickened his step when he saw her, and his face broke into a smile of gratification. He took both her hands and kissed her. 'Ah, I've tracked you down at last, Averil. Your sister told me I should probably find you here. What an elusive girl you are—I haven't been able to get in touch with you at all. I phoned twice last night, and again this morning, but no luck! So I decided, on the spur of the moment, to come down here and see you instead.'

She stared at him for a moment of silent surprise, quite unable to find any reply. For one thing, it was so unlike Kevin to do anything on the spur of the moment. For another, he looked so different. Kevin in Exeter, in charge of his boutique, or at her studio, advising her, encouraging her, was one thing. But Kevin here in Cornwall, in his dark suit, with his crinkly fair hair brushed neatly back, was another. Against a background of high rocks and tossing sea and windswept grasses, he was utterly out of place. Even his voice sounded different here, higher pitched, almost querulous.

She pulled herself together and said, 'What a surprise, Kevin! How did you manage to get away?'

'Half-day closing—had you forgotten?' There was a faint reproach in his tone, as if he had expected her, even when she was away on holiday, to be constantly thinking of him and aware of what he was doing back at home. *And I would have been if I'd been in love with him,* she thought.

'Yes, of course, silly of me.' She pushed back the tangle of bright tawny hair from her face and smiled at him. She must somehow manage to show some pleasure that he had driven nearly a hundred miles on his half-day, just to see her. 'I've been rather caught up in things happening here. One of the guests was taken seriously ill last night—did Sara tell you?—and just now we've been doing a sort of mountain rescue on my young nephew's pet donkey. He strayed out of his field.'

She turned her head to see that Bill had moved away and was untying the improvised sling which still enclosed Methuselah's middle, while the old donkey, quite unperturbed by all the excitement, was quietly munching away at a juicy patch of thistles. 'Bill, this is Kevin Bryant, who sells some of my jewellery in Exeter. Kevin, Bill Randall. Bill belongs to the company that owns the Cormorant.'

Bill strolled across and the two men shook hands. Bill gave Kevin an interested stare, but Kevin seemed hardly aware of the other man's presence.

'And this is Methuselah,' Averil said.

'Oh,' Kevin looked at the disreputable old donkey and his eyebrows rose. 'Oh yes,' he added politely.

There was a lengthening silence. Bill lounged back against the tree, hands stuck deep in his pockets. Kevin fidgeted with his tie, cleared his throat, and finally said, 'We'll find somewhere for tea, shall we, Averil? There's something important I want to talk over with you.' He glanced towards Bill. 'I expect you'll be wanting to get on with your work.'

Averil smothered a laugh. Kevin evidently thought Bill was some sort of handyman in the employ of the firm, one of whose duties was attending to the donkey. And indeed, at this moment he did look rather a ruffian, she thought fondly. Debris of all kinds from the rocks clung to his sweater, there was a dirty streak across his cheek and a gash in his trousers. His dark hair was dishevelled, and damp with sweat.

Also, there was a wicked gleam in his blue eyes. 'I'll see Methuselah safely back to his field, Miss Averil,' he said with a wide grin. 'I have some sugar lumps in my pocket,' he added softly.

'But—' she began uncertainly. It seemed a horrid anti-climax that the risky venture they had just shared should fizzle out like this. On the other hand Bill was quite capable of making Kevin look a fool, which didn't seem quite fair.

'Oh, all right,' she said rather ungraciously. 'Let's go, then, Kevin. And Bill, *please* make sure that Methuselah's safely locked up this time.'

'Trust me, miss.' He touched one finger to an imaginary forelock.

'Oh you—you—' She glared at him helplessly. Then she flounced round. 'Come on, Kevin,' she said, and almost ran ahead of him up the lane.

Kevin caught up with her. 'Who's that fellow, Averil? He's not been making a nuisance of himself, has he? I didn't much like the insolent way he looked at you.'

'Bill Randall?' Her little laugh ridiculed the very idea. 'Good heavens, no! Look, Kevin, we could have tea at the hotel if you like. That would save you doing any more driving.'

'I'd rather go out somewhere where we could be sure to be by ourselves.' He slipped his hand under her elbow. 'I haven't seen you for ages, Averil.'

'Two days,' she corrected, smiling faintly.

'It seems like ages. Isn't there a café up in the village?' And when she shook her head, 'Well then, what's the nearest place? Mevagissey?'

'No,' she said quickly. 'I—I mean, there's prob-

ably somewhere nearer. We could try Pentewan—
there's sure to be a café there.'

But there was nowhere open yet at either of the two
villages they tried and they had to cruise round for
some time before they finally saw a sign saying TEAS
outside a cottage.

'This will have to do,' Kevin said impatiently.
'Anyway, it'll be somewhere to sit down and talk.'

The tiny front parlour was crowded with tables and
chairs, the tea was too strong and the cakes had probably been bought hopefully for last weekend and kept
in a tin since then. Averil was quite surprised that
Kevin didn't seem to notice; usually he was very critical
about such things.

Not surprisingly they were the only customers and
when the stout lady who served them had beamed and
finally departed and closed the door he leaned forward
eagerly. 'I've got some wonderful news. It had to
wait until we were on our own. But first of all, dear,
have you fixed when you're coming back?'

Averil poured tea into thick flowered cups and
passed one to Kevin. She had never before seen him
look so—what could you call it?—so animated.
Usually he had a faintly world-weary manner, which,
as she well knew, concealed a very keen business sense.
But now, something had really turned him on. His
eyes were shining behind their large, thick-rimmed
glasses and even the crinkles in his fair hair seemed to
be throwing out sparks.

'Actually, I haven't thought about it yet,' she said.
'I came down here mostly to see something of Sara, but
she's been so busy that we've hardly had any time
together. There's been rather an upheaval in the
business side of the hotel—it's been bought by a large
company which owns a chain of hotels—and she's a bit

worried about how it will affect her position. I've been looking up old friends, and then there's been this sudden illness of one of the guests—' She was nattering on, which wasn't a habit she normally indulged in, but for some reason she wanted to put off hearing whatever it was that Kevin wanted to say to her.

Kevin had no intention of being sidetracked, however. 'I think you should come back as soon as possible,' he said firmly, and added with a little smile that was full of meaning, ' if you care about your future at all.'

'My—my *future*?' Her eyes opened wide. He didn't mean—he *couldn't* mean this as a proposal of marriage, surely? Not even the methodical and well-organized Kevin could propose like this.

He leaned back in his chair and laughed. ' Poor Averil, I've teased you dreadfully, haven't I? I mustn't tease you any more; I'll tell you my news straight away.'

So it wasn't a proposal! She breathed more easily.

He took a sip of strong tea and said, 'Those brooches you did for me—the coral ones set in silver—I told you I sold them to some Americans, remember?'

She nodded. ' Yes, I'm glad they sold so quickly.'

' Ah, but that's not all,' he said mysteriously, and paused for the words to sink in. ' Yesterday the man came back—the American who bought them. He wanted to know all about them, where I got them from and so on, and if I could get any more from the same source. Naturally I was very wary at first, you have to be careful over such things. But then it turned out that he's in one of the big New York stores—quite a top man, I should imagine—and he would be very interested in having a regular supply of your work. We didn't get down to figures. I told him that I would have to consult you to see if you were agreeable. That was quite a crafty move, don't you think?' He selected a cake with bright yellow icing and cut it neatly in half.

Averil recognised her cue. She ought to be bubbling over with enthusiasm and excitement and gratitude to Kevin. This was what she wanted, had dreamed of and worked for—to make a modest reputation for herself, so that she could count on an outlet for whatever she produced. This was what every craftsman wanted. A week ago such an offer would have filled her head and her heart with delight; her mind would have been seething with new ideas and designs to work out. But now everything had changed. Now she was in love for the first time in her life.

But Kevin was taking a lot of trouble on her behalf and she mustn't seem ungrateful. She opened her mouth to thank him and then she saw that he wasn't really bothered about her lack of response—in fact he probably hadn't noticed it.

'This man—his name's Redman, by the way—is coming in again on Saturday. I told him he could see you then and then he could give you his ideas.'

He smiled at her across the table. 'Poor Averil— I've taken your breath away, I can see that. But there's no need to be nervous; he's quite an approachable type, and you can leave all the business side of it to me, of course. Acting as your agent, you can be sure I'll get the best possible terms for you.' He leaned forward, his eyes alight. 'This could be the beginning of something really big, you know, Averil. For both of us,' he added. He pulled out a pocket diary and turned the pages. 'I told him about eleven on Saturday, so if you come back on Friday at the latest—'

'Just a minute, Kevin.' She spoke for the first time.

'Hmm?' He was making a note in the book.

'I'm not sure that I shall be coming back on Friday.'

He closed the diary and replaced it in his pocket, frowning slightly. 'Well, Saturday morning is leaving it a bit late, but if you made an early start you ought to be able to manage the journey in a bit over three hours. There won't be much traffic at this time of the year. And I could probably contact Redman and put the appointment back an hour or so—'

'You don't understand, Kevin,' she said. 'I mean, I may be staying on here for quite a time yet.' As long as Bill is here, as long as there's the possibility of seeing him, of hearing his voice.

His forehead wrinkled right up to his hairline. Just for a moment the eyes behind the large glasses hardened, then he smiled again. 'You're worried about yourself too, you know. You have considerable talent ful of you to be so loyal. But you owe something to yourself, too, you know. You have considerable talent and flair, and that's far too rare to be allowed to go to waste.'

'But I don't think any talent I have *is* going to waste. I've sold almost everything I've made since I started at the studio.'

'Yes, but this would be something quite different,' he urged. 'This would be on a larger scale altogether. If you were under contract to Redman you would be able to get much higher prices for your stuff. *Much* higher. Fairly soon you'd be taking on an assistant, possibly two, moving to a larger studio—'

'I'm not sure I'd want to—' she broke in, but he wasn't listening.

'Can't you just see it all? Personal displays of your jewellery at all the exclusive stores? Top people paying top prices to wear an *Averil* brooch, or ring, or whatever. Ads in the glossy magazines. Interviews in the national press: *Averil*, the Yves St Laurent of costume jewellery.'

Suddenly he became very serious and, leaning towards her, looking straight into her eyes, he said very frankly, ' I don't want you to think I'm noble enough to forget all about my own interest in this too. As your agent it would be a marvellous break for me, of course. But it's more than that. I feel we would make a wonderful team, both bringing our own special talents to the job, each relying on the other. You do see that, don't you?'

She felt she was being rushed off her feet. It was marvellous, of course, that anyone should think highly enough of her work to make an offer like this, but it had come at the wrong time. She wasn't on the wavelength. She said, with a little smile, ' Kevin, it's all very flattering, and it's lovely of you to come all this way to tell me about it, but you'll have to give me time to take it in. To get my breath back.'

He smiled at her, reassured. ' Of course, dear. I quite realise that you must feel rather overwhelmed by all this, but don't worry about it. Your part in it is just to carry on as usual and leave all the dull business part to me. Now look, I'll have to be making a start back very soon. I've one or two things to attend to before opening tomorrow morning. When I couldn't manage to get you on the phone today I just downed tools and left everything.'

' Yes,' she said, ' it was very good of you.' She just wanted him to go. It was awful to see him sitting there, so pleased and enthusiastic about this, when her own heart and mind were totally absorbed in something quite different, with the picture of Bill down there on the cliff face and with the overwhelming discovery of her own feelings about him.

'Perhaps we ought to go, then,' she said, picking up her bag. 'I'll think it all over and let you know very soon, Kevin, I promise.'

He looked consideringly across the table at her, seemed to be going to say something, and then stopped.

Perhaps he saw that it would be no use trying, at this moment, to put any more pressure on her. So he paid the bill and they went out to the car.

Back at the Cormorant Averil said, 'Will you come in and have a word with Sara, or have a drink before you start back?'

'No, thanks, I mustn't linger. Give your sister my regards, and Averil—' he stopped her as she put up a hand to open the car door '—think over all I've said very seriously, won't you? Give me a ring tomorrow evening to let me know exactly when to expect you back.'

There was a faintly peremptory note in his voice which she didn't at all care for, but she didn't argue, which would only lengthen the proceedings. In all her life she had never longed so intensely, as she did at this moment, to be alone to sort out her emotions.

So she promised, and he leant forward and kissed her lightly before she got out of the car. 'See you very soon,' he said, and the car moved away down the drive.

She stood for a moment, watching him go, the late afternoon sun lighting up the crinkles in his fair hair. At the turn in the drive he lifted a hand in salute, but did not look round; that would have been against the rules of good driving, of course. She smiled faintly and thought, for no reason she could have explained, 'Poor Kevin!' Then she immediately forgot all about him and ran into the hotel and up to her room.

But there was no time to linger here, allowing herself the luxury of dreaming foolishly about Bill Randall. She had promised to meet Mrs Bartram at the hotel in Truro at six o'clock and she would have to hurry if she were going to be there on time. Fortunately she had packed the suitcase earlier, and now she collected it from the Bartrams' room and ran downstairs again. There was no time to look for Sara and tell her where she was going, but she had mentioned it earlier and Sara would probably remember—or else she would take it for granted she was still out with Kevin.

She was carrying the suitcase across the forecourt of the hotel when she saw Bill. His car was parked just outside the garage; the boot was wide open and he was leaning over, arranging something inside it. Her heart gave a violent leap and she quickened her step. More than anything she longed for him to see her and come over, and yet some disturbing shyness swept over her. Her inside felt as if she had swooped down in a lift, and she had an urgent need to get away before he saw her.

But the suitcase was large and before she had it safely stowed away in the Mini he had seen her and was right beside her.

'Hey, where do you think you're going? You're not *leaving*?' He waved a hand towards the suitcase, wedged into the front seat of the Mini. He looked quite dismayed, she noticed with delight.

'Leaving?' she repeated. As always his nearness filled her with confusion and she stammered a little. 'N—no, of course not. That's Mrs Bartram's suitcase; I'm taking it to her in Truro—she's staying there while the Colonel is in hospital.'

The frown disappeared from his face. 'Oh, I see. You had me worried for a moment. I thought the boy-friend might have ordered you back home.'

'He's not my boy-friend, he's my—my agent,' she said shortly. 'And I don't take orders from anybody.'

He was smiling broadly now. 'You look prettier than ever when you're angry,' he said, and he reached inside the Mini and pulled out the suitcase.

'W-what on earth are you doing?' Averil gasped. 'Please put it back. I promised to be in Truro at six o'clock.'

He glanced at his watch. 'All the more reason for us going in my car rather than yours,' he said, and added, 'it goes faster. Come along, hop in.' When she didn't move he grinned and added, 'That's an order.'

'I don't—'

'No, I know you don't take orders from anybody. You've just said so. So what are you going to do about it?'

She glared at him, her cheeks pink, her eyes sparkling frostily. 'I suppose I could fight you for the suit-case.'

'That would be delightful,' he said complacently.

'But as you're much bigger than I am, and a bully into the bargain, I suppose I must accept your kind offer.'

He was looking very intently at her face. 'Do you know,' he said, 'that you've got the most delightful little dimple just beside your mouth. It makes me want to—'

She jumped backwards against the car. 'Bill, no! Not here. And anyway, you've had your reward already.'

'That was just the first instalment,' he assured her blandly. 'Never mind, I can wait for the next one. Maybe it *is* a little public here.'

She tossed her bright hair back and sailed past him towards his car. He followed with the suitcase and stowed it in the boot and climbed in beside her without another word. She stole a glance up at his face as the car swept up the hill into the village. He was looking cheerful and very pleased with himself.

Out on the main road he put on speed and said, ' Is it true what you told me about the boy-friend? *Is* he your agent?'

' Yes,' she said. ' He has a shop in Exeter. He sells quite a lot of my pieces.'

' H'm. So it's just a business connection? *Not* the boy-friend?'

' That's right.' She wondered how to get him off the subject.

He slowed for a crossroad, put on speed again, and said thoughtfully, ' You must be big business to him if he comes all this way to interview you. Or else he's got it in mind to put the agency on a more—er—personal basis,' he added innocently.

' Look,' burst out Averil impatiently, ' do we have to talk about Kevin?'

Bill grinned. ' Not really. I didn't take to the fellow much, anyway. And I thought he gave *me* a very suspicious look down on the cliff there.'

There was silence between them while the speedometer needle crept from sixty to nearly seventy. Averil had never driven as fast as this before. Kevin seldom exceeded sixty; that was, he said, quite fast enough for anyone, even on the motorway. Driving herself in the Mini she had, up to now, kept to a sedate forty-five, and even then she felt she was whizzing along. But with Bill she never had a qualm; he was a superbly confident driver, and this was a car that gave all he asked of it. She sat back and enjoyed every moment.

They pulled up outside the Close Hotel at three minutes to six.

'Thank you,' Averil said. 'I'd have been late if I'd come in the Mini. That was quite a drive.'

He grinned and pulled the suitcase out of the boot. 'The Old Bird can certainly pick a car. She's a beauty.' He touched the silver-grey rear mudguard of the Mercedes lovingly. 'Trouble is he's not fit enough to drive her now. I'll carry the case in for you and then retire and wait outside while you contact Mrs Bartram.'

She smiled at him and the dimple appeared beside her mouth again. 'It's lovely having a chauffeur.'

'My pleasure, miss.' He touched the imaginary forelock again and she said wryly, 'Kevin thought you were the donkey-lad!'

'I hope you didn't disillusion him.' He looked rather hard at her as he carried the case up the steps of the hotel. 'I might have a fight on my hands and he's bigger than I am.'

She looked up to the top of his dark head, judging his height. 'About half an inch, possibly.' Then she looked at the width of his shoulders, the strength of his arms, the springy resilience of a man's body at the pinnacle of physical fitness. 'You'd make mincemeat of Kevin,' she said, and as they pushed through the revolving door of the hotel she thought again, 'Poor Kevin!'

Mrs Bartram had left word that Miss North was to go up to her room when she arrived, so Averil left Bill in the entrance hall and went upstairs. Mrs Bartram was resting on her bed and looked tired, but she greeted Averil with pleasure and couldn't thank her enough for all she had done.

'I've been at the hospital most of the day,' she said.

'The physician there is taking a particular interest in Hugh's case. He's worked out in the East himself and I'm sure we couldn't have a better man. It's a great relief to me. They won't say anything definite, of course—they never will, will they?—but at least Hugh isn't any worse.'

She was *very* comfortable at the hotel, everyone was *most* kind, and there was a retired Naval commander and his wife staying, who seemed *very* nice people and had asked her to join them for dinner. Averil's eyes were soft as she went downstairs again. She hoped that when she was Mrs Bartram's age she would face troubles with such fortitude and good humour.

Bill drove back at a much more leisurely pace than before, and by the time they reached the Cormorant dinner was already being served. Sara was in the dining room when Bill and Averil walked in together and she gave them a quick glance and then turned back to the service trolley. It was evidently turning out a busy evening. Two of the tables were occupied by parties of three and four, respectively. Miss Stevens was in her usual place near the window, with Eliot sitting opposite. When she saw Averil she lifted a hand in greeting and made a sign for her to join them.

Averil turned to Bill. 'Would you rather be at your own table or will you make up a four? I'd like you to meet—'

But she didn't get any further, for Eliot was on his feet, pleasure and surprise written all over his face. 'Well, blow me if it isn't Bill Randall! What brings you to this remote corner of England?'

Bill crossed the dining room in three strides and the two men shook hands enthusiastically. 'Eliot Dunn, of all people! Did you ever get that tent back up again?'

Eliot shook his head, laughing. 'Not a hope! After you left us we found it in shreds, a couple of miles away. Well, well, well, this is a lucky chance, meeting here. Come and sit you down.' He pulled out two chairs and smiled at Averil. 'You'll have gathered that Bill and I have met before. The last time was in Patagonia in the middle of one of those little gale-force picnics they specialise in, in those parts. We were there filming the Magellan penguins, and Bill—'

'I was on my way down to Tierra del Fuego,' Bill put in. 'I'd heard it was the most desolate place in the world and I was determined to see for myself.'

Miss Stevens was transported with delight. 'How wonderful to meet real travellers!' She leaned forward, her eyes shining eagerly. 'Please, please, tell me all about it, both of you.'

Averil went across to Sara, at the service trolley. 'You're busy tonight. Can I help?'

Sara shook her head. 'No, thanks, we're coping. Did you see Mrs Bartram—how is the Colonel?'

Averil told her all she knew, briefly, and Sara nodded. Then she said, 'Where's Kevin? Isn't he having dinner?'

'No, he had to get back. Business to attend to.'

'I see.' Sara straightened a pile of linen napkins and shot her sister a quick glance. 'He came a long way just to see you for an hour or so.'

'That was business too, really. Business is very important to Kevin.' Averil's tone was dry.

Lily's head appeared round the swing door. 'Mrs Bulteel says can you spare a minute, Mrs Tyndall.'

Sara followed her to the kitchen and Averil went slowly back to the table, where Bill and Eliot were exchanging reminiscences, to the obvious pleasure of Miss Stevens, who looked as happy as if they were two of her prize pupils who had just secured scholarships.

Averil listened too, with a curiously intense pleasure. It seemed to her that if Eliot knew Bill, liked him and admired him, which he quite obviously did, then all Sara's misgivings about Bill *must* be unfounded. If Eliot approved of him, then Sara must surely change her mind about him. But of course, there was the point that Eliot hardly seemed to be Sara's favourite person at present. Averil sighed. Oh dear, how complicated everything seemed to be getting, not least for her herself. Her thoughts turned briefly to Kevin, and she felt a faintly guilty pang of remorse. He'd been so pleased and excited about his news, and he had expected her to feel the same, and she must have seemed to him very lukewarm and unappreciative of the trouble he was taking on her behalf. She really must think out the whole situation very, very seriously.

And then Bill filled up her glass with the wine he had ordered ' to celebrate this auspicious occasion ' as he solemnly put it, and he smiled into her eyes with that special look that told her he thought she was wonderful. And she forgot all about Kevin, forgot the probability that Bill made a habit of smiling just like that at any reasonably attractive girl who came his way, and smiled back at him, floating in a warm sea of delight at his nearness.

The travellers' tales lasted through dinner and coffee afterwards. It seemed as if Eliot and Bill could go on swapping places and adventures for years. Averil could have gone on listening to them for years, too, sitting back in her chair sipping her coffee and watching Bill's face—and occasionally Eliot's. The casual diners took their coffee and departed in their cars and still the talk went on. At one point Averil went to look for Sara, taking the coffee tray back to the kitchen as an excuse.

Sara was busy consulting with Mrs Bulteel about tomorrow's menus. Averil waited until there seemed to be a gap in their deliberations and then said, 'Won't you join us for a little while? Eliot and Bill Randall have discovered that they're old friends and they're telling us about their travels. Miss Stevens is absolutely thrilled.'

But Sara wouldn't be persuaded. She didn't even trouble to make an excuse but just said, in rather a harassed way, 'Not now, Averil,' and went off to the office and closed the door.

Averil stood looking after her, biting her lip, and wondering if Sara was ever going to see sense. She glanced at Mrs Bulteel, who was taking off her white coat and hanging it up. 'I shouldn't worry Mrs Tyndall just now, if I was you, Miss Averil,' said that lady, moving back to the table with her slow, stately composure. 'She's got a lot on her mind, she's not herself at all, it seems to me.'

Averil sighed, 'I'm sure you're right, Mrs Bulteel,' and went back to the lounge.

At half past nine Miss Stevens went off to bed and Eliot stood up and stretched himself. 'It's time I went, I've talked myself to a standstill.' Averil saw the way his eyes went to the door. 'Sara's busy, I take it?'

She nodded. 'Too true. She's always busy these days. I've hardly had a word with her since I arrived.'

Eliot frowned, his kind brown eyes meeting hers anxiously. 'She works too hard.' He turned to Bill, still sitting back in his lounge chair. 'Is it really necessary to slave day and night to run a hotel? You're the boss now, aren't you? You should know.'

Just for a second Bill hesitated. Averil had never

seen him at a loss for words before. Then he said, 'That's the trouble, I don't know, I'm only a beginner. But I agree with you, it's not on. I can promise you there are going to be quite a number of changes very soon.'

She waited, hoping he would enlarge on this rather vague statement. But instead he stood up and said, 'Let's see Eliot safely home, shall we? He's been telling me about his cottage, and we're invited over for a nightcap.'

'Cocoa if you like,' Eliot smiled at her. 'Just like old times.' He looked at Bill and added, 'She used to make the best cup of cocoa in the world when she was twelve.'

In the hall Eliot glanced at the closed office door. 'Say goodnight to Sara for me, Averil.'

'Yes, of course.' She wondered how long his patience would last out.

'You'll want a coat,' Bill said, opening the front door. 'There's a nip in the air, as my grandmother used to say.' Outside, the light over the door threw a glow halfway across the gravel sweep; beyond, the night was dark and a cool breeze blew in from the sea. 'I'll be warm enough in the car,' she said.

'No car this time, lady,' he grinned. 'You'll walk and like it.'

'Healthy fresh air,' added Eliot. 'Make you sleep like a top!'

It was all very gay and friendly. Eliot had not brought his car and Bill evidently didn't intend to get his out. They walked along the lane, up the hill through the village, and round the sweep of the cove to Eliot's cottage, three abreast and arm in arm, with Averil in the middle, cuddled in her green woolly driving coat, her head thrown back and the hair streaming away from her face. She felt young and happy and deceptively carefree.

At the cottage Eliot lit the lamps and put a kettle to boil on the camping stove. The fire had burned almost away, but there was still a glow in the grate and a couple of logs and a little coaxing soon brought it back to a crackling blaze. They sat round and drank cocoa, laced with condensed milk. 'Primitive, aren't I?' Eliot said, and Bill sighed and murmured, 'Suits me!'

Averil, from where she was sitting on the hearthrug, saw the two men exchange glances and then Eliot said, 'How will you take to the change-over to a settled existence and an executive suite?'

Bill leaned forward and put his cup down on the floor. 'Frankly, I'm not looking forward to it one little bit. If I hadn't promised the Old Bird and if he wasn't so keen to have me working with him I wouldn't be doing it. At this moment I'd be somewhere in the wilder reaches of the Amazon. Barranco invited me to join his party, but I had to turn it down.'

Eliot whistled softly. '*Barranco?* You move in elevated circles, don't you?'

Bill grinned very wryly. 'It was my first offer—and the last I'll get, no doubt. Barranco can have his pick.'

Eliot nodded sympathetically, 'Tough luck!' He leaned over to knock out his pipe into the fire and then he said, 'Look, if you find yourself with a week or two free in the autumn you might like to come along with my lot. We'd be glad to have you. We're planning a trip out to Argentina again, it's a super spot for birds.'

Bill's eyes were shining. 'That would be grand— I'll take you up on that. I could—' He paused, looking at Averil. 'We're boring you,' he said, but she shook her head vehemently, denying it.

'I'm as keen an armchair traveller as Miss Stevens.' Only it wasn't that, really. It was just that she wanted to know everything about Bill, every tiny little thing. She was in love, and nothing that concerned him was too trivial to be of vital interest to her.

'Only "armchair"?' Bill said quizzically. 'Don't you ever yearn to get away from it all to faraway places and wide open spaces?'

'Me? I—I—' Coloured pictures unreeled in her mind: Herself and Bill on some lofty height, with a strange magnificent panorama spread out below; trekking through jungle country; shooting the rapids; crossing the Pacific on a raft. All the exotic travel films she had ever seen on television sprang into vivid life as she put Bill into them. Bill and herself, of course. She giggled. 'I've always rather fancied I'd like to see the Grand Canyon.'

'Done!' Bill thumped his fist on the arm of his chair. 'I shall take you there this summer.'

They all laughed heartily, Averil most of all. Next summer, she thought, I shall be working away in my little studio over the hardware shop, and Bill will have forgotten all about me. And how long, she wondered, with a sudden sharp pain in the region of her heart, will it take me to forget him?

Suddenly she scrambled to her feet. 'I think I must be getting back now.' She picked up her coat from the window seat where she had tossed it when they came in. 'Don't you bother to come yet, if you'd like to stay and talk some more with Eliot,' she said, not looking at Bill. Now that the moment had arrived, the prospect of walking back with him, just the two of them in the darkness and the starlight, set up a panicky feeling inside.

He got out of his chair. His head almost reached

to the ceiling of the tiny cottage room. 'Don't be silly,' he said mildly. 'Look, you've got the sleeve inside out—' as she was struggling to get into her coat. He straightened it and helped her into it, his hands resting for a moment on her shoulders and her skin prickled all over.

'I really shall be all right,' she argued weakly. 'I'm quite used to looking after myself.'

'Not when I'm around,' Bill said, and that was that.

He opened the door and let in the cool night air. They thanked Eliot for the cocoa and he said to Bill, 'I'll be seeing you tomorrow then?' and Bill replied, 'I'll look out for you.' They had evidently arranged something together for tomorrow. Averil felt a pang of acute disappointment. If she went back to Exeter on Friday, as good sense told her she should, then tomorrow would be her last day here—and Bill was going somewhere with Eliot. She didn't know exactly what she had expected or hoped, but suddenly the air seemed chillier, the night darker.

They waved to Eliot and he closed the cottage door and they were alone together. Bill said, 'Let's walk back across the beach. The tide must be just about half way out, so we can get round that way, can't we?'

At this side of the cove the cliffs were grass-covered, with a narrow path winding steeply down to the beach. There was no moon, but the light from the cottage threw a faint glow, and they scrambled down, Bill going first so that he could reach up a hand to steady her when the going got particularly rough. At last they reached the damp, furrowed sand from which the tide had recently retreated. 'All right?' Bill asked, and she replied, 'Yes,' suddenly breathless as he tucked his hand in the crook of her arm.

They walked along the edge of the tide, where thin

white waves curled over each other, dragging back with a faint hiss to leave a trail of seaweed and broken shells behind.

Bill waved his hand across the dark swelling water to where a bulge of rock stood out, faintly showing against the sky. 'I suppose that's this Starry Rock that Eliot was telling me about? He's very excited about some visiting bird he's spotted there. He wants to try to film it.'

'The greater yellow-legs. From North America,' Averil recited solemnly, and then laughed, 'See how well I've been trained! I used to tag round after Eliot when I was a schoolgirl. I thought he was marvellous. I still do, for that matter.'

The obvious answer to that was some teasing remark, but Bill didn't make it. Instead he said slowly, 'I think he's marvellous too. I ought to, because if it weren't for Eliot Dunn I probably shouldn't be here tonight.'

'He—he saved your life?'

'Eliot would laugh that off, but all the same that's what it amounts to. I'd been damn silly enough to venture into a particularly unhospitable part of Patagonia alone. The man I was with had broken his leg and had stayed behind in Buenos Aires, getting it better, but I was keen to push on south, so I did. I was over-confident I could make it on my own. I asked for trouble, and I got it.'

'What happened?' Averil asked in a small, wondering voice.

'What always happens in those parts, apparently, sooner or later. The wind got up. I'd been warned about it, of course, but I didn't realise what wind means out there, with mile upon mile of—of *nothing* all around. It must be one of the bleakest, most godforsaken spots in the world. Once the wind starts to blow it can go on for days, and it carries everything with it if you're not prepared—and even if you are, sometimes. The first day it ripped my small tent to pieces, and soon after it disposed of most of the rest of my gear. The final insult was when it got my water container and bashed it against something sharp—a bit of rock, I suppose—and I found that my precious supply of water had almost trickled away.' He laughed ruefully. 'In those circumstances you go a little crazy after a while. Incessant wind is very lowering to the morale. I must have been wandering round for quite some time when Eliot and his crew spotted me and took me in. They were better prepared—and more sensible. They had one tent undamaged between four of them, and they shared what food and drink they had left with me. Then we just sat it out until the wind dropped. I can't remember how many days it was.' He was silent for quite a time, looking out over the sea as they strolled along. 'So you'll understand,' he said at last, 'why I was so pleased to meet up with old Eliot again. He's a grand chap.'

'Yes,' said Averil softly. 'Oh yes, he is.'

By now they had reached the bottom of the steps leading up to the cliff top at this side of the cove. He released her arm to let her go up first, but kept his hand on hers. 'You and Eliot—you're not—?'

She laughed. 'I love Eliot dearly—as a brother. Or—hopefully—as a brother-in-law. Only there seem to be so many snags,' she added on a little sigh as they began to climb the steps.

They both fell silent as they walked along the lane up to the hotel. It was very dark here, between the high banks on either side. At the gate leading into Methuselah's field there was a shadowy bulk and the

sound of steady munching. 'He's none the worse—
he hasn't lost his appetite,' Averil said. She swung
round. 'Oh, Bill, I really am grateful to you for this
afternoon. If you hadn't been around he might
have—'

'But I *was* around.' They stood by the gate, and the
silence that followed his words began to feel as if it
were loaded with a high electric charge. She was dis-
turbingly aware of his body, so close to hers, and her
senses swam with a warm delight as she felt that in a
moment he would pull her into his arms and kiss her
as he had done before. The darkness seemed to vibrate
with the urge of spring, of growing things forcing their
way up through the earth. The stars were thick
clusters, sprinkled across the black velvet sky, and from
somewhere near came the plaintive squeak of some
small night bird. So strong was the tension that almost
she turned into his arms, buried her head against his
shoulder. Her heart was thudding so hard that she
was sure he must hear it.

Then he said, as if there had been no silence at all,
'—which makes it all the more sad that I have to go
back to London on Friday.' He turned his head towards her. 'Will you miss me, Averil?'

For a brief, idiotic moment she wondered what he
would say if she told him the truth: *When you go the
world will stop.*

But a light question demanded a light answer.
Somehow she managed to say, 'I'll be simply heart-
broken. But I'm going back to the job myself on Friday, as it happens, so I'll have to bury my grief in
work.'

With an enormous effort she managed to persuade
her legs to start walking up the lane again. It would
be terrible if he thought she had been lingering there

by the gate, expecting him to kiss her; the fact that it was true made it all the more humiliating.

He had been straight with her from the beginning. She was to be a diversion to save him from the boredom of beginning in a job he didn't want to do. He wasn't, as he had carefully assured her, the settling-down type. Oh yes, he had played the game according to the rules. It had been her own stupid fault if she had fallen in love.

He fell into step beside her, but he didn't link arms in the old easy way. He said, conversationally, 'You've got a lot of work on hand at present?'

'Absolutely snowed under,' she said brightly. 'I shouldn't really have stayed away so long, if it hadn't been for Sara. She's been a bit under the weather lately. I think she's worried.'

'Yes, I know,' he said in the serious voice that seemed unusual from him. 'I promised you I'd do my very best to see she's all right, and I will, Averil.'

'Thank you,' she said.

They had reached the front door of the Cormorant by now. In the bright light over the door Bill's face looked strangely pale. If *he* looked pale then she herself must look positively ghastly. She shivered and said, 'I must ask Sara to put a less stark light up here. This one's too unflattering for words.'

He looked at her and said, 'I shouldn't bother. You still look very beautiful.'

She wished he would go back to his old teasing tone. It made things so much worse when he sounded almost as if he were serious.

The light in the hall was mercifully dim. Averil glanced at her watch and said, 'I think I'll go straight up to bed. Goodnight, Bill.'

'Goodnight, Averil.'

He didn't watch her go upstairs. Even without looking she knew that he was walking away, and when she glanced down from the top of the stairs she saw him going into the telephone room.

To ring Louella, no doubt. Would they talk business, or had their relationship already gone far beyond that, as his grandfather planned? Well, it had nothing to do with her. Nothing, nothing, *nothing*!

She went into the bedroom and closed the door and she was thankful that Sara wasn't there to witness the tears that flooded into her eyes before she could stop them.

CHAPTER VII

Bill met her at the bottom of the stairs next morning as she came down to breakfast. He was wearing a shirt and tie today, under a tailored jacket, and she guessed he was going up to the north coast to join Louella. Her heart sank still further towards her shoes.

'Hullo, you're late down.' He sounded unbearably pleased with life.

'I'm afraid I overslept.' She struggled to produce a smile. It had been a horrible night. The effort to appear normal by the time Sara came to bed had been prodigious, and the nervous tension involved had kept her awake for hours. In contrast Bill looked particularly buoyant as he said, 'I'm off up north now. Louella has finished the job she was doing at our hotel there, and she's going to give me the final run-down on what she's decided. I'm on a watching brief just now, as I told you, but I'm learning fast.'

Averil said politely, 'I'm sure Miss Andrews is very capable.'

He glanced sharply at her. 'Oh yes, she's a clever girl, our Louella. But I didn't want to talk to you about that. I wanted to ask you if you're free later on today. Eliot is coming up to Padstow to see the " Obby Oss " festival. It's a new one on me, but he says it's part of our ancient heritage and shouldn't be missed. He's well up in all these things. We've arranged that he'll come back to the hotel for dinner—it's not far from Padstow. Will you join us and make a party of it?'

Life came back, bubbling through her like champagne. She would be near him, be able to look at him, talk to him. And even if the snooty Miss Andrews was there too, it was much, much better than nothing.

'Thank you, I'd like that,' she said. ' I've never seen the " Obby Oss " thing. I've always meant to go, but I've never quite managed it. I did go to see the Furry Dance at Helston—or the Floral Dance, as some people call it.'

He grinned and said, ' That's a much more civilised affair, I believe. The " Obby Oss " really keeps its earthy flavour, I understand from Eliot, so we can all let our hair down. I'll drop in at Eliot's cottage now, and ask him to pick you up after lunch. That suit you?'

She nodded, her eyes shining. ' Yes.'

For a moment he stood looking at her, in her green trousers and jumper, with a string of carved wooden beads round her neck and the morning sunlight striking bright glints from her hair. ' Until this afternoon, then,' he said, and went out to his car.

Averil made for the kitchen. She had planned to skip breakfast, but now she suddenly felt ravenous. Sara was conferring with Mrs Bulteel; when she had finished she saw Averil and came over to her.

'Hullo, dear, you were having a lovely sleep, so I didn't wake you. I thought you seemed tired last night. What would you like? There's plenty of porridge left, and bacon, but no kidney, I'm afraid. I was just going to have something myself, so let's eat together.' She loaded up a tray and carried it to a table in the empty dining room.

'Miss Stevens is having breakfast in bed,' Sara went on, 'and the Randall man has handed in his key and left. He told me that he's staying tonight at the hotel near Padstow, and is going back to London tomorrow. I can't say I'm sorry to see him go.' She sat down and began to pour out coffee. 'I suppose I'll just have to wait now, and see what happens. He didn't give me a clue. It's all been rather mysterious, the way he came here. He said he was learning the business, but really he didn't seem very interested in what was going on here.'

When Sara talked about Bill they were on different wavelengths entirely. Averil poured cream carefully on to her porridge and said, 'I'm going up to the "Obby Oss" festival at Padstow this afternoon. Eliot is calling for me.'

'Eliot?' Sara put the coffee pot down with a little clatter. Her brown eyes opened wide and her lips parted. She stared blankly at her sister, and Averil thought: It is true then, you *can* read emotions on people's faces. In that unguarded moment Sara was registering shock in no uncertain fashion. Something else too, that looked very like jealousy. It was a complete giveaway. She *did* care about Eliot, still, in spite of the way she behaved to him.

Averil went on calmly, 'Yes. It's Bill Randall's invitation, really. We're going to see the festival and then have dinner at the hotel. Miss Andrews will be

144

there too.'

Sara let out her breath. 'Bill Randall? Oh—oh, I see.'

Averil applied herself to her porridge with appetite, leaving Sara to get her bearings back. Finally she became the elder sister again. She looked at Averil rather anxiously and said, 'Are you sure you're wise to go?'

'Wise?' What had wisdom to do with the way she felt about Bill? She shrugged. 'Probably not. We're not very wise, are we, when—' She stopped.

Sara said, 'You're in love with the man, aren't you?'

There was a little silence. Then, 'I'm crazy about him,' Averil said, and admitting it aloud to someone else made the whole thing more real—and more hopeless.

Sara nodded. 'I see. Is he—is it serious, or mustn't I ask?'

Averil smiled. 'I said crazy, didn't I? It's serious for me, but it's not serious for him. He made it quite plain the first time we—talked that he isn't the settling down type. You know: "Warning. Proceed beyond this point at your own risk." Well, that's what I did, and today I'm going to live for the moment, because I've got to go back to my work in Exeter tomorrow.'

'And Kevin?' Averil heard the eagerness behind the enquiry. Sara would be thankful to see her comfortably settled with a man like Kevin, someone solid and dependable.

'I don't know,' Averil said. 'Maybe, maybe not.'

Their eyes met across the table, and perhaps Sara saw the determination in her young sister's face. She sighed and said, 'I haven't forgotten what it feels like to be crazy about a man, you know. I just hoped that you would be spared the heartache.' She stood up, giving her shoulders a little shake. ' I'll go and get the bacon. Oh, and I must tell you, I had a letter from Adrian this morning. He's been put into the form team and he's thilled to bits about it. I'll show you the letter.'

By the time they had finished breakfast, and Averil had read Adrian's letter, and Sara had talked proudly about her son and his achievements, it was after ten o'clock. They went into the office and Sara telephoned the hospital, to be informed that Colonel Bartram had had a comfortable night, and that his temperature was lower this morning.

' That's wonderful,' Averil said. ' Mrs Bartram will be so relieved. I must try to see her again before I leave.' Saying that reminded her that today was the last day of her strange little holiday, the last day she would see Bill. She changed the subject quickly, looking at the pile of unopened mail on the desk. ' I suppose you're going to be busy this morning?'

Sara looked at the pile too. ' It looks like it. What are you going to do?'

' Wash my hair and dream about this afternoon.' There was a touch of bravado in her voice which she hadn't intended. She felt a stab of remorse. Sara loved her, she knew, and only wanted the best for her —just as she wanted for Sara. She said, ' I'm so glad we had time for a bit of a talk at last, Sal. I wish—' No, she mustn't bring up the subject of Eliot.

Upstairs, she washed her hair and dried it with Sara's hair-dryer, sitting at the window and looking out over the low green hills behind the hotel, and wondering what she would wear this afternoon. She would wear the Aztec dress for dinner, but it would hardly be suitable for wandering round the streets of Padstow, probably in a strong breeze. It would have

146

to be her green trousers, but she could change the green jumper for a white angora one with a soft turnover collar, and the necklace of linked copper that looked nice with her hair. She could pack the Aztec dress, and take it with her, to change at the hotel.

When her hair was dry she brushed it into a chestnut sheen, and leaned closer to the mirror to inspect her reflection. Not bad, she decided. She would never compete with someone like Louella Andrews for sophisticated style and the kind of grooming that comes out of Vidal's or Leonard's. But all the same—not bad!

She remembered Bill's voice last night saying, ' You still look very beautiful.' Not to be taken seriously, of course. Nothing about Bill Randall could be taken seriously, except his courage, his devil-may-care, offhand, amazing courage. Thinking of him on that sheer, jagged rock, taking that risk just to rescue an old donkey, still made her shudder, and at the same time glow with admiration.

She recognised the imminent danger of wandering off into a daydream, so she stood up resolutely, picked up her coat, and went downstairs to the telephone. For once in her life she was going to be sensible and organised.

Kevin replied to her call in the precise voice he always used in working hours. When she had checked that she wasn't interrupting him in any possible sale, she told him that she had arranged to return tomorrow morning.

' Tomorrow—Friday—ah, yes. Just a minute, Averil.' She pictured him picking up the pencil, making a note neatly on the pad beside the telephone: ' Averil—Friday, 2nd May—12 p.m.' Kevin never doodled at the phone, as she did, and his notes were always legible and economical.

'Good,' he said briskly, and she felt that he had never seriously doubted that she would do as he wished. 'I'll get on to Redman and arrange for you to see him and show him some more of your work. Either tomorrow afternoon or Saturday morning, whichever suits him best. He's flying back to New York on Sunday, I understand. I'm glad this is all fixed up, Averil. You won't regret it, I'm sure, and—' he hesitated for a moment '—I was thinking we could have dinner out somewhere tomorrow evening, to celebrate your success and cement our new partnership.'

'Oh, well, thank you, Kevin. We'll arrange something when we meet, shall we?' Just at this moment she couldn't commit herself any further.

'Will you come straight to me here when you arrive? I'll be glad to know you're safely back.'

She laughed. 'You don't trust my driving, do you?'

He said seriously, 'This hasn't anything to do with your driving, Averil.' There was such a long pause that she thought they had been cut off. And then Kevin said, very softly, 'I want you back with me, my dear.'

This was straight talking, and no mistake. She didn't know what to say, so it was just as well that he didn't wait for a response, but added in his normal voice, 'There's a customer just come in. I'll ring you later and tell you what I've arranged with Redman.'

She said, 'Make it before lunch, Kevin. I'm going out this afternoon.'

They said goodbye and she went to look for Sara in the office. 'May I interrupt you for a moment?'

Sara looked up, smiling. 'Of course.'

'I wanted to tell you that I've decided to go

148

back to Exeter tomorrow morning. I've just been on the phone to Kevin to let him know. He's going to ring me back later on, and I thought perhaps you wouldn't mind taking a message if I'm not in?'

'I'll do that,' Sara said. She looked pleased and expectant and Averil thought, I may as well tell her now. 'Kevin has found an important possible buyer for my jewellery. Apparently he may offer me a contract, which may lead to something quite big. Kevin wants me to see him before he leaves for America on Sunday. That's why I'm going back tomorrow.'

Sara looked surprised and delighted. 'Why, of course you must go! This is simply wonderful news, love, the reward for all your years of work and study. Why didn't you tell me before? Was that why Kevin came down to see you yesterday?'

'Well, it wasn't really fixed up and I wanted to wait and be sure before I said anything about it.' She wished she could tell Sara the whole truth: that beside the earth-shaking fact that she had fallen in love with Bill Randall everything else had paled into a vague shadow. But she didn't want to wipe the pleasure from Sara's face, and that statement surely would.

'I'm absolutely thrilled,' Sara said, 'and I'm sure you are too. It's what you've always wanted, isn't it, to be able to go ahead and concentrate on your work without having to waste time looking for buyers. Aren't you excited?'

'Yes, of course.' She did her best to sound enthusiastic, but it wasn't easy. Perhaps when she had finally said goodbye to Bill and knew that she wouldn't be seeing him again, her life would slot back into its old groove. If what she felt for him was just a physical thing it could be short-lived if you were sensible about it. Everybody said so. But she kept remembering the terror and the agony she had felt when he was hanging by his fingers and toes on that cliff, and that emotion didn't seem to have much to do with a simple sex attraction.

She left Sara to her work and walked up into the village. She had to find out how Methuselah's gate had come to be left open yesterday, and make sure it wouldn't happen again. She walked round the side of the whitewashed Ship Inn and knocked at the back door. Mrs Ellis was working at the kitchen table, making pasties for the bar. The Ship did a good trade in pasties, both in and out of season. The youngest Ellis boy sat in a large wooden chair near the stove, his podgy legs stuck out in front of him, his small mouth sulky. A crooked, somewhat grimy bandage was fixed round his head and the red hair spiked out around it.

'What can you do with 'em?' sighed his mother, when she had greeted Averil. 'I'm only out for about an hour yesterday, having my eyes tested. I leave young Tim to look after the two little 'uns. And when I come back, here's this young man with a two-inch gash in his head. Rob had to leave off his work to take him in to have it stitched. Now he's feeling very sorry for himself, aren't you, Lionel?'

Lionel stuck out his lower lip and maintained silence. 'He wants to go out to play, but he can't, not today.' Mrs Ellis's look softened as it rested on the fiery small head. 'It was while he was out playing yesterday he got this lot. Fell and cut his head on a stone, Tim told me. Tim was properly upset when I got in—you can imagine. He's a good lad, and grown up for his age, or I wouldn't have left him, but he couldn't cope with Lionel bleeding like he was, and he was a bit scared to go and tell his dad what had

150

happened in case his dad blamed him for it.'

Tim had evidently not told his mother the whole story, but Averil thought she could reconstruct it now. She could imagine Lionel falling off Methuselah's back and cutting his head, and Tim, in a panic, rushing him home and leaving the field gate open. He wouldn't tell his mother or father exactly what had happened, in case a veto was put on any further donkey rides.

'Tim's at school this morning, is he?' she enquired casually, and Mrs Ellis, pushing a batch of pasties into the electric oven, nodded. 'Doing quite well too, his teacher says.'

'That's splendid,' said Averil, deciding there and then that the details of yesterday's accident might well be kept between herself and Tim. The tough young Lionel was just as likely to collect the usual crop of cuts and bruises whether he indulged in any further donkey rides or not. She would make a point of seeing Tim and warning him about the gate, and that was probably all that was necessary.

As it happened, she met Tim in the village, on his way home from school, almost as soon as she had said goodbye to his mother. 'Hi, young Tim, I want a word with you.'

He stopped immediately, turning a deep red below his freckles as he recognised her and put two and two together.

'I've just been to see your mother, Tim,' she said.

He shuffled his feet and stared down at the road. Then he lifted his head and met her eyes. 'Did you tell her—'bout us riding the donkey, miss?'

He was quick on the uptake; no wonder his teacher was pleased with him. 'No, as a matter of fact I didn't,' Averil said. 'But I'd like to hear just what happened—from you, Tim.'

He looked relieved. 'I was giving Lionel a ride, miss. You saw us when you went past the gate, didn't you? Well, a bit after that he was, you know, being sort of silly and showing off and—well, I dunno quite how it happened, but he fell off and he must have hit his head on a stone or something, 'cos he was bleeding something awful. I got a proper scare.'

'You must have done, Tim,' Averil said quietly. 'What did you do?'

'Lionel was bawling like mad and he wouldn't stop, so I picked him up and carried him back home. William was crying too, by that time, but I couldn't bother with him, so I just told him to shut the gate and come along.'

'You carried *Lionel*—all the way up the hill?'

Tim grinned. 'He was a bit heavy, miss, but we got back somehow, and then Mum came in—and it was all right.'

There was a pause and at last Averil said, 'And that was the whole story?'

He looked a little sheepish. 'Well, not exactly, miss. You see, after Dad had taken Lionel to the hospital I began to think, and I wondered if our William had closed the gate properly, so I went back to look and—and—the gate was open and the donkey wasn't there.' He bit his lip and she thought he was going to cry, but he gulped and battled on. 'It was awful. I went down the lane to look for him, and then I saw him with this man. I thought he'd tear a strip off me when I told him 'bout leaving the gate open, but when I 'splained how it happened he said I wasn't to think no more about it. And he gave me some money to buy Lionel some sweets when he got back from the hospital.' A delighted, almost awed grin spread across the thin freckled face. 'Gosh, he's *super*, isn't he, miss?'

Averil smiled back warmly. 'Yes, I think he's super too, Tim,' she said, and on that note of agreement they parted and went their separate ways.

Averil walked on through the village and along the headland path to Eliot's cottage, but Eliot wasn't there. From high up she could see straight across to Starry Rock. The tide was nearly full and the sands were covered by sea. She could make out Eliot's small dinghy moored in a tiny sheltered inlet; and right at the top of the Rock she saw a slowly-moving bright blue patch, which was no doubt Eliot's windcheater. He was probably on the track of the greater yellow-legs again. She hoped he wouldn't get too carried away to remember that he was supposed to be calling for her right after lunch.

She scrambled down the grassy track and walked across the crescent of beach left by the tide. Back at the hotel Sara was standing at the outside door of the sun lounge. 'I've been looking everywhere for you, Averil. Kevin has just been on the phone, and he wants you to ring him back as soon as possible. He said it was urgent, and he wouldn't leave a message.'

'Oh dear, what now?' said Averil, and went into the small telephone room.

Kevin answered so quickly that she guessed he must have been waiting near the phone. 'Averil? Oh, good! Look, my dear, our plans have changed somewhat. I've been in touch with Mr Redman and he has to fly back to New York earlier than he expected. The only time he can possibly see you is this evening, about seven o'clock. I'm sorry to rush you like this, but if you start out quite soon you can make it easily. Come straight here to me, will you? I've arranged that we shall all meet here and then we can go round to your studio together when Redman arrives, and take it from there. All right?'

She reacted as she always did to Kevin in this mood. She stiffened all over. She said quietly, ' I'm afraid it isn't all right, Kevin. I'm already booked for this afternoon and evening; I think I told you.'

' Then I'm afraid you'll have to put it off. You can explain how it is.'

' I'm sorry,' she said, ' but I can't put it off.'

' You *can't*?' he echoed unbelievingly. ' Averil, I don't think you know what you're saying. This is business, it isn't just a holiday outing. What, for goodness' sake, could be more important than the whole of your future? *Our* future,' he added, with an emphasis that left no room for misunderstanding.

' I'm sorry,' she said again, ' but you see, I promised.'

' But surely you can explain to—whoever it is. You can't let me down like this, it would make me look such a fool. I told Mr Redman you would be delighted to come here to meet him. What do you imagine he'll think?'

' You could take him to the studio yourself,' she suggested. ' You could show him anything he wants to see just as well as I could. You could probably do it better, come to that.'

'Oh no, that wouldn't do at all.' His irritation was growing now as it began to dawn on him that she might just possibly mean what she was saying. ' You're the one who is going to do the work for him. If he thinks you're not sufficiently keen to go to a little trouble to keep the appointment—'

' That isn't fair,' she broke in. ' I'd promised to come back tomorrow to meet him, that was the original arrangement. It's Mr Redman himself who has altered it.'

'But he's an important man.' Kevin was obviously keeping his patience only by the greatest of efforts. 'You have to be prepared to put yourself out if you want to get anywhere with a man like that. I can't seem to make you understand—'

'But I do understand. I understand very well,' she said.

'Then you'll come?'

'I'm sorry,' she said once again. 'I can't.'

His self-control left him. In a kind of vicious exasperation at her stubbornness he burst out, 'Look, Averil, you're behaving like a fool. You *must* come back.'

Unconsciously she lifted her chin a little. '*Must*, Kevin?' she said very quietly.

Perhaps, all those miles away, he heard the crackle of ice in her voice and realised he had gone too far, for his tone softened as he said, 'Yes, I really think you must. It means so much to our future together. To all my plans—'

Quite calmly she said, 'Kevin, I'm afraid I really don't think we have any future together of any sort. This has made it quite clear to me.'

There was a long silence. Then he said, 'You mean that?'

'Yes,' she said.

Another pause, then she heard a click at the other end of the line. Kevin had hung up.

She replaced the receiver carefully and stood looking down at it, seeing nothing. After a time she went out into the garden and did some deep breathing to quieten the nervous tumult inside her. Sara found her there a few minutes later. 'Lunch is ready,' she said. 'Will you have it with Miss Stevens in the dining room?'

'I'd rather not, if you don't mind,' Averil said. 'I'm feeling a bit shattered at the moment—I've been having a showdown with Kevin on the phone. Would it be all right with you if I put something on a tray and take it upstairs?'

Sara gave her an anxious look. 'Yes, of course. I'll get Lily to take a tray up to the bedroom for you, and you can have it there in peace and quiet.'

Averil looked gratefully at her sister. 'Thanks, you're an angel.' Then, as Sara turned away, she said impulsively, 'Sal, you may as well know—it's all off with Kevin.'

'All off? You mean—'

'I mean everything. He wanted me to rush back to interview this man from New York this afternoon instead of tomorrow as we'd arranged. Apparently his plans have changed and he has to fly back to New York earlier than he expected. I told him that I couldn't come, that I had already got something fixed for this afternoon and evening, and he was absolutely furious. He tried to—to pressurise me into changing my mind, and that was fatal.' She grinned wryly. 'You know me, Sal, I can be led but not driven. And Kevin is the driving kind. It would never have worked out.'

Sara looked distressed. 'Averil, love, I'm terribly sorry this has happened.' She put a hand rather diffidently on Averil's arm and her sister gave her a warm, grateful smile, and said,

'Don't be, Sal. In a way I feel relieved. Things could have drifted on between us—you know how it is—but it would never have been really right. The longer you go on the more difficult the break is, when it comes.'

Sara nodded. 'Yes, well, I'm glad you feel that way about it. Just for the moment I thought you might have refused because of—'

'Because I wouldn't give up a date with Bill Randall?'

'Yes.'

Averil laughed and hoped it sounded convincing. 'That would have been pretty feeble of me, wouldn't it? To let a wonderful opportunity go just for the sake of seeing a man for the last time.' If she said it often enough, thought it often enough, she might come to believe it. To hope for anything more than the most casual and fleeting affair with Bill would be sheer lunacy, and she knew it.

Suddenly she didn't want to be alone. 'I think I'll change my mind and join Miss Stevens for lunch after all,' she said.

Eliot called for her just before two. He waited in the hall while Averil went to find Sara, to say she was going. 'Come and see us off,' she said, and, when Sara drew back a little, she took her arm firmly and Sara had to go.

Eliot's approach to Sara was different today; he seemed a little offhand. He said, 'It would have been nice if you could have got away from the old grindstone long enough to come with us and join in the fun,' but he certainly didn't seem unduly disappointed. He took great care to see that Averil was comfortable in the front seat of his low, wicked-looking coupé. It was a funny thing about Eliot—he didn't seem to match his car at all. He gave the impression of being the mildest, quietest person in the world. But his choice of car was anything but mild. There were, Averil thought sagely, many hidden depths in Eliot.

He switched on the engine and, putting an arm around Averil in a way which wasn't altogether brotherly, he smiled at Sara and said, 'I'll bring her back safe and sound, but I won't make any promises about *when*.' Then, lifting a hand in salute he reversed the car expertly and drove off with a spatter of loose gravel and a good deal of style. Averil, looking back, saw Sara standing quite still, watching the car as it disappeared.

They joined up with Bill's car outside Padstow. He was waiting in a lay-by, evidently by pre-arrangement with Eliot. He jumped out of the car and joined them. Averil's heartbeats quickened as he stood looking down at her in the sunshine. He had changed the formal clothes he had beeen wearing earlier, and in a thick jersey, his dark hair ruffled by the wind and his eyes as blue as the slit of sea in the distance, he looked absolutely breathtaking, she thought besottedly.

'I've just been in the town,' he told them. 'The processions are getting under way again. Apparently they have a lengthy stop for liquid refreshment in the middle of the day. I've been finding out all about it. There are two processions and two Osses, the Old Oss and the Blue Ribbon Oss. They keep on different routes until this evening, when they meet and dance together. And there's a maypole and a fair and the fun gets even more fast and furious. They're living it up fairly well now. Just listen.'

They all stood still and listened. From the direction of the town came the sound of drums, of singing, and the music of the band. Bill said, 'Come on, let's go and take a look. It's absolutely stunning, I promise you. Oh, and by the way, we'll have to get along without Louella.' He chuckled. 'She took one look at the crowd and suggested that I run her back to the hotel, which I did. The Obby Oss isn't quite her sort of thing—not civilised enough. We'll have to walk from here; there isn't a square inch of parking space left in the town.'

They locked the cars and swung along the road, Averil between the two men, an arm linked with each. The sun shone and the air was crisp and clean—and Louella Andrews wasn't there. All causes for joy!

' Tell us about the origins of the festival,' she said to Eliot. ' You're the expert on these things.'

' No expert,' he protested. ' But these old festivals have always intrigued me. It's extraordinary how they crop up all over the world in very similar forms. Have you come across any in your wanderings, Bill?'

' As a matter of fact, I have,' said Bill. ' When I was in New Guinea I saw the natives perform a sort of masque, which reminded me of what's going on here. As soon as I saw it today I remembered.'

' There you are, you see.' Eliot nodded. ' Strange, isn't it, how primitive people everywhere seemed to hit on the same ideas, long before there was any telly or newspapers to link countries and continents together. Though I suppose it's not so strange, when you come to think about it. They're all concerned with the same basic things: birth, and life, and death. The sun rising and setting. The seasons following each other. The Obby Oss probably began as a pagan festival of revival and fruitfulness—the earth being reborn after its winter death, and bringing forth its bounty. The ancients were very close to nature. They felt themselves to be part of it in a way that we, now, have forgotten how to do. All these old ceremonies and festivals and rites were their way of helping the processes of nature along.' He chuckled as he added, ' Many of them were pretty elemental, but they've been censored and watered down and made more "respectable " as the centuries passed.'

'What a pity,' remarked Bill wickedly, and they all laughed.

Happiness bubbled up inside Averil. 'Come on,' she cried, 'I can't wait to see it!' And she began to run.

The small town wore an air of gay festivity. The streets were decorated with bunting and greenery and the crowds milled everywhere, some obviously local people upholding and enjoying their own festival, others visitors with cameras slung over their shoulders. A group of women pushed Averil and the two men forward, saying goodnaturedly that they had been out all morning and had seen the procession before.

Soon a ripple of excitement passed through the crowd as the sound of singing and music came nearer and nearer, and eventually the procession came into sight, led by a tall man in tails and top hat.

'Oh look,' Averil gasped in delight. 'There's the Oss. Isn't he simply marvellous?'

The Obby Oss was an amazing and quite terrifying creation. On his shoulders he carried an enormous hoop, which must have been nearly six feet across, like a huge black dinner plate. From this hung a cloak of black canvas which reached down to his knees and revealed legs encased in white trousers below. On his head was a tall witch's hat with wide stripes and below that a ferocious mask with whiskers. A young man in white danced round the Oss, carrying a short padded club, with which he seemed to conduct the Oss's movements. He and the Oss performed a curious dance together continuously, like a quaint *pas de deux*. The rest of the Oss's party were in white too, some in sailor suits with cowslips and tulips stuck in their hats. Some played drums and accordions, cymbals, tambourines, and they sang as they went—one of those lilting, monotonous tunes that go on, verse after verse, apparently for ever. The crowd joined in the singing too. It was all delightfully uninhibited and unselfconscious. The only words that Averil could make out were the ones repeated at the end of each verse: ' In the merry mor-*ning* of May,' and she joined in with all the rest.

The procession had reached them now, the Oss reeling and capering from side to side, like a small craft on a choppy sea. Then, before she had time to register what was happening, the strange beast darted across the road towards their small group. Perhaps the Oss had caught a glimpse of Averil, in her spring green coat, with her bright hair, and decided that here was a likely candidate to carry on the life cycle. She found herself grabbed and enveloped in the black swirling cloak. For a moment she was held prisoner there, in the dark, while the crowd cheered and shouted some words she couldn't make out. Then she was released into the sunshine again, laughing breathlessly in confusion.

It was impossible not to feel slightly embarrassed, but the feeling evaporated in the spirit of goodnatured revelry all round. The women nearby were laughing, and one of them said meaningly, ' You'm lucky, m'dear,' and Eliot grinned and interpreted, ' She's saying that you've been specially chosen to carry on the human race.'

' Oh, dear, and I'm not even married!' wailed Averil. She put a hand distractedly to her hair, and Bill laughed and pulled her against him and, to the obvious delight of the women, declared, ' Oh, we'll soon put *that* right.'

All foolery, of course, and yet there was something about the old rites that gripped you. She looked up uncertainly at Bill and his face was serious now, his eyes slits of intense blue under their long lashes. The noise and the crowded street seemed to fade away and they were the only two people in the world.

Eliot's voice jolted her back to reality. 'That was quite a performance. The old Oss has very good taste. Now then, how would you like to fill the rest of the afternoon? Perhaps you two would amuse yourselves together for a while? I'd rather like to look up a fellow I used to know who lives a few miles inland from here.' He glanced from Bill to Averil. 'Two's company, so they say. You'll excuse me?'

Bill grinned at him. 'We wouldn't dream of stopping you.'

It was arranged that they would join up again at the hotel for dinner. Bill provided directions, and Eliot went off. 'That man has tact,' Bill remarked appreciatively. 'Now we have the rest of the afternoon to ourselves.' He gave her a teasing look. 'Can you bear it?'

Our last afternoon together—and the end of the romantic interlude! Every minute bringing nearer the inevitable parting, when she would drive away with Eliot and her world would be empty because Bill wouldn't be in it any longer.

Stop it! she screamed silently at herself. She had known from the first what the score was, that for Bill she was merely a pleasant way of helping to pass a few days which would otherwise have been rather a bore. He had said as much and she had accepted it, so she mustn't start moaning now and feeling sorry for herself. And she must take good care not to show him that the interlude meant anything more to her than it did to him.

So she smiled gaily at him and said, 'I'll just have to try to bear it, won't I?'

162

He linked his arm with hers and led her away from the crowded streets. 'I suggest we get in the car and go exploring,' he said, and Averil agreed. She didn't mind what they did, just so long as they were together with something to do, something to see, something to share. That way she could almost pretend that she would see him again tomorrow—and the next day—

So they set out along the coast road southwards, stopping the car whenever they felt inclined, to wander down inviting ways to the sea. Later in the season the beaches would be full of people, if the summer turned out kind, but now they were empty, just stretches of golden sand enclosed by towering black headlands, with always the white-crested waves rolling in from as far out as they could see.

They stood on the edge of the tide and Averil said, 'I can never believe that the waves don't actually travel along, although we learned at school that they're caused by the water just going up and down. I'm sure some of these waves came all the way from America.'

He said, 'Good for you. Never believe all the scientists tell you. It takes all the romance out of life.'

'Don't tell me you believe in romance.' She laughed up at him. 'You, a hard-bitten traveller!'

'Ah, but travellers are all romantics, although they might not admit it. Always looking for the marvellous, exciting places at the end of the next trek—or flight—or voyage—'

'Tell me about some of them,' she said, and he linked his arm with hers, and as they walked he told her of forests and swamps and deserts; of mysterious ruined cities; of ancient temples; of fascinating and sometimes dangerous beasts, and exotic flowers.

'I don't wonder you didn't want to come back to civilisation,' she ventured at last. 'Do you think you'll settle down to it?'

He stopped walking and looked far out to sea, his eyes suddenly puzzled. 'Don't let's talk about it,' he said. 'Come on, let's go and explore some more.'

They drove through Newquay and Perranporth, then turned inland and circled back. At Bedruthan Steps they parked the car on the turf and made their way to the edge of the cliff, looking down at the beach far, far below. So far below that Averil felt giddy and was glad there wasn't time to climb down all the hundreds of steps to get to the beach, where fantastically shaped granite rocks reared up, just like the giants' stepping stones that legend supposed them to be. It was wild up here. The wind roared and buffeted them, bent the stunted trees back double and flattened the sea grasses.

'Reminds me of Patagonia, and that time with Eliot,' shouted Bill. 'Only—' The rest of the sentence was inaudible.

'Only what?' She had to say it twice before he heard.

'Only it's much nicer here with you,' he yelled back, and they both saw the ridiculousness of a compliment hurled through the screaming of the elements, and collapsed with laughter.

It was a gay, thrilling afternoon, but all too soon it was over and they got back into the car to make their way to the hotel. Averil sank into her seat and opened her handbag. 'Do you mind if I do some running repairs? I can't arrive looking like a wreck from the sea.'

He lay back in the corner of the driving seat, watching her while she struggled with the tangles. 'You look delightful,' he said softly, and suddenly she was overcome by the most appalling shyness and could not meet his look.

'Don't try too hard,' he said. 'You're not really an every-hair-in-place girl.'

'Aren't I?' She glanced up innocently.

He did not move, but once her eyes had met his she could not look away again. The space between their two bodies seemed to tingle with their awareness of each other. Averil held her breath, acknowledging that it was for this moment that she had waited; for this moment she had turned down the career chance of a lifetime.

'You're so sweet, Averil,' he murmured huskily. 'So very sweet.' And he moved nearer on the wide front seat of the car and took her in his arms. She felt the hard thudding of his heart as he held her close, the roughness of his cheek as it pressed against hers. Then his mouth found her mouth, and she closed her eyes. The kiss went on and on—

The splutter of a car engine brought them back to reality as a small family saloon drew off the road and parked almost alongside. The elderly couple inside looked across at them and smiled amiably.

'Damn!' exploded Bill. 'They have the whole of Cornwall to choose from, and they have to stop here!'

Shocked back into the world of everyday things, Averil laughed helplessly. 'And faced with the most superb scenery in the whole country they have to get out their newspapers,' she said, as they did so.

Bill glowered. 'It isn't funny,' he said darkly, as Averil went on laughing. Her laughter was more than half hysteria but he didn't seem to notice that, for presently he grinned reluctantly and then he was laughing with her. After that the spell was well and truly broken and Bill started up the car and drove back on to the road. 'Other times, other places,' he said.

'And other girls?' she murmured. She couldn't help it. But he didn't rise to the bait. He turned and gave her a look which she couldn't interpret, and then he put his foot down hard on the accelerator.

It was a fitting end to the disturbing wildness of the afternoon, with its tossing sea and keen, gusty wind, and the crying of the gulls, and the white puffy clouds scudding across the blue sky. Bill drove at a rate which made her clutch the edge of the seat, until she realised that he knew exactly what he was doing, and began to enjoy it.

All too soon he turned off the main road and, a couple of minutes later, pulled up before a low white building fronted by a perfectly-trimmed lawn. There were no gates but a small board announced discreetly 'The Cliff Hotel. One of the Raven Group.'

As they went inside Averil realised just what Sara had meant about Raven Hotels. Nothing could have been less like the homely old Cormorant. Here was super-luxury, super-service, super-everything. 'One of the Old Bird's more successful ventures, I understand,' Bill murmured as he put a hand under her elbow and led her across the foyer into a lounge with a long picture window overlooking a sweep of sea. He installed her in a chair as soft and downy as a dream. 'I'll go and find Louella, and see if Eliot has turned up yet. Would you like a drink now, or wait until we all get together?'

She said she would wait, and watched him walk across the lounge away from her, thinking that in a way he was already walking out of her life. Already, in these surroundings, he had become a different man. The Bill who had run across the sands hand in hand with her; the Bill who had risked himself to save an old donkey out on the cliff; the Bill who had drunk cocoa, sitting on the kitchen table; that Bill had gone, and in his place was this tall, distinguished, almost arrogant stranger. The man she had first seen at the garage outside Bodmin had come back, and she felt she didn't know him at all.

As she sat and waited the life of the hotel throbbed round her in a muted kind of way. Stewards in short white jackets served drinks to the elegant guests. Conversation rose and fell languidly. Oiled lift gates clacked softly. A telephone buzzed and was answered immediately. The smell of cigar smoke and French perfume was wafted gently on the warm, conditioned air. Oh yes, she saw just what Sara meant now. To manage an hotel of this class you would need special training, special qualifications, which Sara hadn't got. Depression settled inside Averil, and she began to wish she had never seen this place. It would have been so much better to say goodbye to Bill up there on the cliffs, with the wind blowing his dark hair and the sun making his eyes glint with blue fire.

But there was no getting out of it now. They were coming across the room towards her, Bill and Louella, and she thought dismally that they made a wonderful pair. Bill, even slightly dishevelled as he was by an afternoon in the open air, was easily the most distinguished man in the room. And Louella, in a black silk trouser suit, her pale hair swept up into an intricate knot, was the picture of sophisticated poise. She greeted Averil charmingly, scolding Bill for leaving her without a drink.

' You poor child, you must be simply exhausted. All the bucolic goings-on at Padstow! Not my sort of thing at all, is it, Bill darling?' She gave him a ravishing smile.

'Not in the least,' he said, and smiled back at her in an easy, intimate way that made Averil's fingers curl into her palms.

'Come along up to my room and tidy up, and I'll have them bring a drink to you. What do you fancy?'

Bill said, 'Averil prefers to wait until we're all together,' and Louella's beautiful eyebrows lifted in faint surprise.

'Really? Well, order me a brandy, darling, while I take her upstairs.'

'Eliot's arrived, he's brought your case with him,' Bill said, as they reached the foyer. A diminutive coloured boy in uniform appeared by the lift, with Averil's case, and opened the gates for them.

'See you later,' said Bill. As the lift started its ascent Averil couldn't look at him, for she was afraid his smile would be for Louella.

The room that Louella took her into was as luxurious as the rest of the hotel. Averil felt she should say something appreciative. 'I'm very impressed by the Cliff,' she said, opening her case and shaking out the Aztec dress. 'You wouldn't think of a hotel like this tucked away in a remote place like—why, I don't even know if it's marked on the map.'

Louella's smile was faintly superior. 'Why, that's the whole idea of the Raven Hotel Group,' she explained kindly. 'Perfect service in perfect places, away from the pressures and chaos of city life. Our guests are top people who expect the very best—and get it.'

'But isn't it rather far from London? The travelling—'

'Oh, we have our own airstrip. Most guests come by private plane.'

'I see.' Averil was feeling more out of her depth

every moment. She didn't doubt that there was a place for hotels like this, but she found the prospect of the Cormorant being given a high gloss infinitely unattractive.

'I suppose there will be changes at the Cormorant, now that your group has taken it over?' She didn't expect that Miss Andrews could tell her anything that would allay Sara's fears, but at least it might be better to know the worst. And as Bill couldn't—or wouldn't —talk about it—

Her thoughts came to an abrupt stop at the amused expression on Louella's face. 'Oh no, that's not the idea at all. Mr Raven didn't buy it as a hotel. It will be closed down at the end of the season.'

'Closed down?' Averil stared at her blankly. 'But —but *why*?'

Louella looked faintly bored. 'I understand that Mr Raven intends to use it as a country residence— after alterations and redecorating, of course.'

Averil had a heavy, desolate feeling inside. It was awful to think that the Cormorant wouldn't be home any more. Even worse to contemplate the effect this would have on Sara. And there was something else that was worse, even, than these. She lifted her head slowly. 'Does Bill know about this?' she said.

'Well, of course he does.' The other girl gave her a patronising stare. 'That was mostly why he came down here, to look the place over and give his grandfather a report on its condition. Mr Raven bought it from an old friend of his, I understand, and knew the place years ago, when it was a private house, but naturally it will need a great deal doing to it to bring it up to Mr Raven's standard.'

'Oh, naturally,' murmured Averil automatically.

She didn't notice Louella going out of the room.

Hardly knowing what she was doing, she washed and brushed her hair and did her face and got into the Aztec dress.

Bill knew about the Cormorant. He had known right from the beginning and he hadn't told her. Even when they talked about it, when she told him how much the place meant to Sara and to her, he had kept quiet. Probably he thought her stupidly sentimental and had been afraid she would make a fuss if he told her the truth. Perhaps he and Louella had laughed about it together. A fire began to burn dully in her cheeks.

Sara had been right about him all along, and she had been wrong. She had fallen in love with him like a romantic schoolgirl, and she had endowed him with all the virtues. She had thought him kind and sensitive as well as strong and dashing and brave. She had kidded herself that she had his friendship. And he hadn't cared enough about her to tell her the truth, that was what hurt most. He had promised to 'look after Sara's interests'. No doubt that was because he was bored with the whole matter and wanted to get out of it in the easiest possible way.

Well, at least she knew the truth now, and the sooner she said goodbye to Bill Randall and started the task of forgetting him the better. Meanwhile there was this dinner to be got through, and she wished with all her heart that there wasn't.

It was quite dark, nearly two hours later, when Bill walked with Averil and Eliot to Eliot's car, but the Cliff was brilliantly floodlit from end to end. Eliot unlocked the door and put the two cases in the back and then said, ' I've just remembered I've left my watch in your room, Bill. I'll go back and get it. And I've got a phone call to put through too. Mind waiting a jiffy, Averil?'

Left alone with Bill, she plunged into words. 'Thank you for a lovely dinner. It was super.' She heard her voice, high and unnatural. Her face felt stiff with the long effort to smile all through the meal, to look as if she were enjoying every minute of the superbly cooked and served dinner. 'In fact, the Cliff is super altogether, isn't it?' she ran on. 'Very different from the poor old Cormorant.'

There! She had given him a last chance to tell her. It wouldn't be too difficult for him now. *Look, Averil, before you go there's something I should have told you—*

But he leaned a hand casually on the bonnet of Eliot's car and said, 'Oh, I don't know about that. I like the Cormorant. It's got a lot to be said for it. A resident donkey, for instance.'

Why did he have to say that? Why did he have to look down at her so intently in the soft back-glare of the floodlights? Still in that high light voice she said, 'That's another thing I have to thank you for—that Methuselah's there still, I mean. And I've enjoyed our outings together and—and everything.'

He was smiling now. 'Yes,' he said softly, 'I've enjoyed it too. Especially the everything.'

Her pulses began to throb. Even now—even when she knew he would probably have forgotten her existence an hour from now, the old magic was still there. Both the men had changed for the evening, and in his dinner jacket Bill had looked devastatingly handsome, but she had been almost able to persuade herself that he was some stranger who had joined their party. She had almost believed that the Bill who had rescued Methuselah, the Bill in the grimy torn sweater and earth-streaked face, the Bill she had fallen in love with, had been another man altogether. But now she knew it wasn't going to be as easy as that. She wanted to cry, but instead she said, 'You and Louella are going back to London tomorrow?'

'At the crack of dawn,' he said. 'Urgent matters of state to attend to. Oh, goodness, I nearly forgot, you never gave me your phone number in Exeter.' He groped in his pocket. 'Damn, my notebook's in my other coat. Have you anything to write it on?'

The old, old thing. They said, *I'll ring you soon*, and you hung around the phone, waiting and waiting. But that wasn't for her; she was her own girl. ' 'Fraid I haven't,' she said, and added, 'anyway, I'm going to be quite desperately busy when I get back.' That sounded just right, she thought with bitter satisfaction. Friendly and regretful, but quite, quite final.

There was a long pause. Then he said in an odd voice, 'You mean that? Really?'

'Yes, really. I've got a rather important contract coming up.' She wasn't a girl who lied easily and that hurt.

'Ah, yes, I'd forgotten. You told me how much your work means to you. I shall keep my eye open for an Averil North exclusive. Cuff links, perhaps.'

She laughed. 'Yes, you do that.'

Eliot was coming across the grass towards them. 'Ready for off?' He looked uncommonly cheerful, for some unknown reason. Bill opened the car door for her and she hesitated for a moment. Then she held out her hand. 'Goodbye, Bill.'

He took her hand and drew her to him and kissed her deliberately. 'Au revoir,' he said. And he almost pushed her into the car and closed the door on her.

CHAPTER VIII

They were speeding along the main road before Averil
could get control of the tears that blinded her, blurring
the approaching car headlights into swimming streaks
of brightness. She dug her fingernails into her palms
and clenched her jaw until it ached. She wouldn't for
the world embarrass Eliot, who could not have any
idea how things stood between herself and Bill. After
Bill's leavetaking Eliot probably imagined they had
made plans to meet again. That was the impression
anyone might have had. Anyone but Averil herself,
who knew just how much it meant. Before Louella's
disclosure, she thought, she would have been building
castles in the air now, believing he really meant 'au
revoir' and not 'goodbye'. But now she knew him
better. He was a man who used all his charm to avoid
any situation which might turn out awkward for him.
She tried to hate him and instead found herself working out excuses for him.

Eliot's voice broke in on her self-absorption. 'I
gave Sara a ring just before we left,' he said casually.

'Oh?' It came out as a strangled choke, but he
didn't seem to notice.

'Yes, just to warn her that we were leaving, and to
expect us in an hour or so. She said—' a smile crept
into his voice ' —she would have coffee and sandwiches
waiting for us. For *us*,' he added meaningly. 'Do
you see what that means? For the first time she has
actually issued an invitation, of sorts, to me. I could
almost believe I discern a crack in the ice.'

'Oh, I do hope so.' Averil forced herself out of
her private misery. 'You know, when you called for

me this afternoon, I thought she looked—it probably sounds absurd—but I thought she might be a tiny bit jealous that it was *me* going off with you in your car.'

She heard his chuckle in the dim light. 'I must confess that the same possibility occurred to me too. Keep your fingers crossed for me, little one.'

'Oh, I will,' she promised fervently, and she meant it more than ever. If Sara married Eliot then it wouldn't matter that she was going to be out of a job at the end of the summer.

Then another thought struck her. Whatever happened she mustn't tell Sara what she had found out about the Cormorant closing down, because if she knew, and knew that Eliot knew, she would probably retire again behind her stiff barricade of pride, imagining that he was asking her out of pity. Averil sighed. How complicated everything was! And how much easier life would be if only people could be straightforward with each other!

As she had promised, Sara had coffee and sandwiches waiting in the small private sitting room behind the office. The curtains were drawn and chairs pulled up to the electric fire, where a tray was set on a low table. It looked cosy and comfortable, if perhaps—after the magnificence of the Cliff—a little shabby. But it was nice, and it was home. Averil blinked away the tears that would keep coming into her eyes.

Eliot sank into a chair. 'This is delightful, much better than the Cliff.' He must have noticed the contrast, too. He pulled out his pipe and looked at Sara. 'May I?'

'Of course.' Sara raised her eyes from the coffee tray hardly far enough to meet his. She was wearing the mink-coloured jersey dress with the gold belt and there was a tinge of pink in her cheeks tonight. She looked very pretty, Averil thought, and as shy and uncertain as a young girl. And the chill had gone from her manner when she spoke to Eliot.

'How was the Cliff?' she asked, pouring out coffee. 'Tell me all about it.'

It was Eliot who replied. 'Oh, very, very glossy. A little of that sort of place goes a long way with me.'

Sara nodded. 'I thought it might be like that.' But she didn't sound too depressed.

Averil sipped her coffee and nibbled a sandwich and felt it would choke her. Eliot was talking about the Obby Oss, and suddenly she was back in Padstow and Bill was standing beside her, and she couldn't stay here a moment longer.

She got to her feet. 'Will you both forgive me? It's been quite a day, and I've got a splitting headache. I'll take myself off to bed. No, don't bother to come up with me, Sal. I know where you keep your aspirins. Goodnight, Eliot, and thanks for taking me. It's been a—l-lovely day.'

Her mouth began to tremble and she made for the door and stumbled blindly up the stairs. She wasn't going to cry if she could help it; you felt so awful afterwards. As she undressed, she clenched her jaws until they ached. She swilled her face, cleaned her teeth, and opened the dressing-table drawer for a hand-kerchief. There, on a little wad of cotton wool, was the yellow shell brooch that Bill had bought for her in Gorran Haven.

The tears had their way then, and she dived into bed and pulled the bedclothes up over her chin. And while she wept she faced the bleakest thing of all. In spite of her brave words to Sara, in spite of convincing herself that she knew what she was doing, she hadn't really believed that Bill could go out of her life like this, as casually as he had come into it. All the time, deep down, she had been wishing and hoping, fooling herself that if you wanted something badly enough, longed for it deeply enough, you got it in the end.

It's your own fault, she accused herself. All that grand stuff about doing it your way and taking the consequences! You'd have done better to listen to Sara at the start. But you can't go moaning to Sara now, because she's just beginning to surface again herself after all these years.

Tomorrow, she told herself, it would be better.

But of course it wasn't. In fact, it was worse, because she had to get back to the business of living without the prospect of seeing Bill.

Sara was busier than ever. She was expecting an intake of visitors on Saturday, and many more the weekend after. The season was beginning to get into its swing.

'Will it be all right with you if I stay till Sunday?' Averil asked her. 'It's a bit depressing in town at the weekend, on one's own.' Previously she would have seen Kevin and they would have talked about her work and the boutique, and perhaps have driven out into the country, but not any more. Kevin reckoned that she had let him down and he wouldn't waste any more time on her. Business meant more to Kevin than any girl ever would. She supposed that after a while they would have to meet again, but it would be strictly on business. Anyhow, that was how she wanted it.

'Of course, my dear, stay as long as you like. I love seeing you around. I only wish we could have more time together, but you know how it is.' Sara was different this morning, more relaxed, and the look she gave Averil was warm and affectionate. 'You all right?' she added.

'I'm fine,' Averil said, and smiled brightly—too brightly perhaps, for Sara gave her a quick glance, but said nothing. 'I'll go back to Exeter on Sunday afternoon, then I can get ready to start work in earnest on Monday morning.'

It was funny how endless time seemed when you were unhappy. Friday and Saturday were the two longest days of Averil's life. She did her best to fill them up. She went for walks. She cleaned and polished the Mini. She chatted to Miss Stevens. She drove over to Truro and saw Mrs Bartram and found that the Colonel was making good progress now, and that all being well they hoped to let him out of hospital early next week.

'We should both so like to come back to the hotel for a while,' Mrs Bartram said. 'That is, if your sister can put up with us. We shouldn't be any trouble. I could take Hugh's meals up to him and look after the room and so on. Do you think she'll have us? I'm afraid we've been rather a nuisance to her already, and she has been so kind and thoughtful.'

'I'm sure she will be glad to have you back,' Averil said, 'and you mustn't feel you've been a nuisance. I know Sara doesn't feel that at all.'

Mrs Bartram sighed with relief. 'I've stayed in many hotels in my time, but never one like the Cormorant,' she said warmly. 'You don't expect that kind of consideration.'

They had tea together at a little cake shop in Truro, and Mrs Bartram talked of her life abroad, in faraway places. That reminded Averil of Bill again. Everything reminded her of Bill. Everywhere she went, in the hotel, out on the cliffs, on the rocky beach, talking to Methuselah, Bill was everywhere.

177

On Saturday evening Eliot came to dinner again. Later, he persuaded Sara to go out with him for a walk on the cliffs, and she allowed herself to be persuaded, to Averil's delight. There were six new guests, and she might have made that an excuse to refuse, but she didn't. She said to Averil, as Eliot waited by the door, 'Won't you come, too?'

'Sorry,' Averil said. 'Miss Stevens has promised to teach me how to play piquet,' and she watched the two of them go off together with an enormous sense of relief. At last it looked as if Sara was going to be happy.

Averil played piquet with Miss Stevens until that lady said, with reluctance, that it was her bedtime. Sara hadn't returned, so Averil watched TV with some of the new arrivals. It was an old film, a war story, and the man went off to the Western Desert and left the girl to carry on at home, and it was all poignant and understated and Averil found herself nearly weeping again, so eventually she went off to bed. When Sara came up, much later, she pretended to be asleep.

After lunch on Sunday she packed her case and carried it down to the hall. Sara met her there and tried to persuade her to stay another day, but Averil had made up her mind. 'I'll just go over to the cottage and say goodbye to Eliot and then I'll be off. I'll see you before I go, of course.'

She felt that she was holding out on Sara by not telling her what she had found out from Louella Andrews about the Cormorant's future. She would have liked to ask Sara straight out whether she was going to marry Eliot, but of course she couldn't do that. He might not have asked her yet. But if she saw Eliot herself she might find out. It would be lovely to be able to feel really happy about Sara before she left.

She ran across the beach to the cottage. The tide was low and the sands washed into clean yellow furrows. She paused for a moment to look at it and her heart ached. The beach had been ' her ' place since her childhood, and now, whatever happened, it would not be ' her ' place any more. When the Cormorant was no longer itself, but Mr Matthew Raven's country residence, she didn't think she could bear to come back.

She climbed slowly up to the cottage. There was no answer to her knock and she waited for a while, then pushed open the door and went in. The remains of breakfast were on the table, and the dishes in a bowl in the sink. She washed them up and cleared the table, but still Eliot hadn't come back.

She waited another few minutes and then, disappointed, wrote a little note for him, left it on the table and went out again. He was probably over at Starry Rock, watching the greater yellow-legs. He was planning to try to film it, she knew. He had been telling Miss Stevens about it at dinner last night. She looked across the expanse of wet sand, to the Rock in the distance. If she could be sure he was there she would walk across and say goodbye, but it was quite a way to the Rock and back, and she didn't want to be too late starting on her drive to Exeter.

Then, as she looked, she saw a tiny splash of colour near the top of the Rock and recognised it as Eliot's bright blue windcheater. She hesitated, thinking that if she were late starting off on her journey she might have to finish the run in that half-light which is so confusing for new and inexperienced drivers. But the wish to find out how things stood between Eliot and Sara was too much for her. She pulled off her shoes and socks and rolled up the legs of her trousers, and began to run across the wet sand.

Starry Rock was, perhaps, a quarter of a mile off shore, but Averil covered the distance in a sprint and sank down, panting, when she reached the tiny inlet where Eliot usually moored his dinghy. It wasn't there now, but of course it wouldn't be, because he must have walked across earlier, while the tide was still well out.

He must be somewhere up there on the top of the Rock, and she was about to call to him when she saw the greater yellow-legs. He was standing just above her and she recognised him immediately: the white upper rump, and long, slightly turned-up bill, and of course, the stilt-like yellow legs that gave him his name. She froze into stillness, remembering, from her earlier excursions with Eliot, how fatal it was to move or make a sound. Eliot must have a hide somewhere and at this very instant he was probably engaged in photographing his quarry. He would never forgive her if she spoilt it for him.

Minutes passed and Yellow-legs stayed where he was. For a while she was fascinated and admiring, for he was very beautiful, and she noticed how the other seabirds kept their distance. Perhaps, she thought with a smile at the fancy, they were being polite and deferring to a visitor from overseas. But soon she began to get impatient. She lowered her eyes to her wristwatch, but it was hidden by the sleeve of her jumper. Time must be getting on, and she was beginning to regret her impulse in dashing over here.

She eased her aching legs, fractionally, into a more comfortable position, keeping her eyes on Yellow-legs all the time. He was preening now, stretching his wings, digging under his feathers with that long bill, taking his time over the business, now and then stopping to bob his tail in a quaint way. She sat on, silent and unmoving, hoping that Eliot, at least, was getting some satisfaction from the performance.

Over and over again, her mind turned to Bill. Bill, who was so entwined in her memory with this place, with the sea and the rocks and the yellow sands. Once she got away, she thought, she wouldn't come back to Cornwall for a long, long time. Perhaps never.

There was a whirr of wings as Yellow-legs took off and she breathed a sigh of relief. Now she could call to Eliot, could climb up to find him. But after circling twice the bird alighted again in the same spot and began, presumably, to look for food, prying his bill into the crevices of the rock. Eliot would enjoy that, no doubt.

Averil glanced a little anxiously at the stretch of sand between her and the mainland. It would be most uncomfortable to be cut off on Starry Rock while the tide came in and went out again. She made a quick assessment and reckoned that the tide must be on the turn any time now. Very soon she would *have* to move, Yellow-legs or no Yellow-legs. In any case, Eliot would have to emerge soon, as he hadn't got his dinghy with him. She listened, trying to hear the faint whirr of the camera, but there was only the sound of the wind rising. But of course Eliot was much too experienced a naturalist to let his camera action be audible. He would have it muffled in some way. He must be pleased with the pictures he was getting. She only hoped he wasn't so pleased that he wouldn't notice the tide.

The wind was stronger now. It was chilly, too, and she wished she had brought a coat, but of course she had intended to be away for only a few minutes. A strand of hair escaped from its scarf and flicked her cheek, then the tip of her nose. Her arm twitched instinctively, but earlier training with Eliot restrained it from moving. Fatal to move your hand when there was a bird in sight!

A tickle that you hardly notice when you are busy quickly becomes intolerable when inactivity makes you focus your attention on it. Averil sat in increasing anguish while the thin strand of fine hair flicked against her nose with what almost seemed like deliberate malice. She gritted her teeth and stuck it out. Seconds passed like centuries. The itching became worse and worse, gradually getting more intolerable until it filled the whole of her consciousness. More time passed. Then—Forgive me, Eliot, but even for you I can't—bear it—any—longer—

Her hand went up and swept away the strand of hair, to her exquisite relief. At the same moment there was a magnificent flapping of dappled wings, and Yellow-legs rose in the air and soared away into the distance.

She didn't wait to see if he would return. She got up stiffly and shouted, 'Eliot—Eliot—where are you?'

There was no reply except the cry of the gulls. 'Eliot!' she called again. Then she pulled on her shoes and began to climb over the rocks, up to the spot where she had seen his blue windcheater. Now that she had suffered all this, she had no intention of leaving until she had found him.

'Eliot!' Starry Rock was higher than she remembered and the lower part was slippery, but she climbed on, gradually reaching the margin of seaweed that marked high water. He *must* be up here somewhere. That bright blue patch she had seen couldn't have been anything but Eliot's windcheater.

She levered herself up a little higher and then she

saw it. It was indeed Eliot's blue windcheater, but the ridiculous thing was that Eliot wasn't inside it.

She could have wept. She had been crouching here in—to put it mildly—some discomfort all this time and Eliot hadn't been in action at all. No filming of yellow-legs. No necessity for all that uncomfortable effort to keep dead still. 'Bah!' breathed Averil in disgust. Then, because it really was rather funny, she began to laugh. And what, in the name of bird-watching, was Eliot's windcheater doing up here? He might be a little absentminded about things like clothes, but surely—

She eased sideways to examine it. He had left it there on purpose, no doubt about that. It was wedged between two rocks, and one sleeve was anchored by a stone. Oh well, she thought, these mad naturalists! And, still chuckling, she moved to climb down again, feeling for a foothold below.

Perhaps if she hadn't been laughing, if she had been concentrating on what she was doing, as all good climbers should, it wouldn't have happened. As it was, her lower foot seemed to swing out into empty space. She clutched wildly at the windcheater with her free hand and it came away from the rock where it was wedged. Unbalanced, she fought to hang on with her other hand, struggling for a foothold. Hazily she thought, *Bill should be here, he wouldn't let me fall.*

It was probably the windcheater that saved her. When she had the strength to straighten herself out she found that she was lying on a ledge some six feet or so below, still gripping the sleeve of the wind-cheater. The other sleeve had hooked itself on to a spike of rock and held fast, breaking her fall. Gingerly she flexed her arms and legs, and explored for possible damage. Blood was seeping from a cut on her ankle and her hands were badly scratched. She'd been lucky, she thought, looking down at the twenty feet or so of black rock below her.

Some time passed before she felt strong enough to climb down to the bottom, and when she reached the inlet the worst had happened. The tide, blown by the wind, was rushing in strongly, curling across the sand. From experience she knew that already the wide, deep channels would be full. If she wanted to get back now she would have to be prepared to swim for it.

'I can't,' she said aloud, suddenly weak. 'I'd never make it.' She would just have to stay here until somebody realised where she was.

Time dragged. It seemed like hours, but she couldn't know because her watch had shattered in the fall. She kept her eyes glued on the strip of beach on the mainland. Surely Sara would begin to wonder why she was away so long, and go over to Eliot's cottage to find out?

Clouds blew up, the sun went in, and Averil began to shiver. As the tide rose she had to climb higher. The Rock was never completely covered, even at high spring tides, but it would be a most uncomfortable place to spend the night on.

She was beginning to calculate how many hours it would be before the tide was low again, and coming up with the answer of three in the morning, when she spotted something moving on the beach. Two tiny figures —Sara and Eliot, she guessed, though it was impossible to recognise anyone at this distance. She stood up and waved. 'Stop! Please stop, I'm here!' But the words were carried away on the wind and the two figures moved on, climbed the grassy cliff and disappeared into the cottage.

Tears of disappointment welled into Averil's eyes and

she brushed them away with grimy, bloodstained fingers and began to wait again.

Then Eliot emerged from the cottage alone, and stood looking out—she thought towards the Rock. She pulled off the windcheater and waved it high above her head. She went on waving, wildly, desperately.

Eureka! He had seen her. He was running down the path, across the beach, pulling his small rowing boat to the edge of the water, drawing out the oars.

The boat skimmed over the water. Twice he glanced round to check his direction, then pulled strongly on the oars again. He was nearly in now and she hobbled out to the edge of the lowest rock that was above the water line.

The boat eased in, stern first. 'Mind how you go, Eliot!' she shouted. 'Rocks just below water here!'

He shipped his oars and grabbed the nearest hand-hold, then tossed a rope round a protruding spar and drew it fast.

'Eliot, how glad I am to—' She stopped, struck dumb as the man in the boat turned and stared up at her, at her face streaked with blood and grit.

'My darling girl,' said Bill, horrified, 'what on earth have you been doing to yourself?' He climbed out, took her gently into his arms and kissed her cold, salty lips. 'It's just about time I came back to look after you. No, not a word—' as she began to stammer out something almost incoherent, in her amazement—'I'm going to get you back as quickly as possible.' He got back into the boat and held out his arms. 'Can you manage to climb in? Hold on to me, I won't let you go.'

Never let me go, never again, thought Averil. Never go far away from me. And she slid down into his waiting arms like a child coming home.

*　　*　　*

It was heavenly warm sitting in Eliot's cottage, wrapped in Eliot's camel dressing gown, with a steaming hot cup of tea beside her. Averil smiled up at the still faintly anxious faces around her and said, 'I feel a bit like Grace Darling, rescued from the sea. Only she was a heroine and I've just been completely foolish.'

Sara threw another log on the crackling fire and said, 'It must have been ages before I realised that you hadn't come back. I was busy after lunch in the office. Then Bill arrived and we—talked.' She threw a friendly glance at Bill, on the other side of the fireplace. 'And then suddenly I noticed what the time was and knew you should have been back long before. So Bill and I went over to Eliot's cottage to see what was happening. He wasn't there, but we saw your note, and then we began to get really worried, I can tell you.' Sara still looked pale in the dancing light of the fire. 'You'd put the time on the note—three-fifteen. By then it was nearly half past five.'

Averil grinned at her. It was easy to make a joke of it now, with her ankle and hands bathed and bandaged, and a good lacing of Eliot's best brandy in her tea. 'Did you think the piskies had got me?'

Sara didn't see the joke. She said, 'I think you can imagine what I thought.'

Averil could. Last year a woman visitor had fallen over the edge of the cliff not very far away from here. She had been middle-aged and a stranger, whereas Averil was young and knew the place by heart, but Sara wouldn't have considered that. And anyway, for all her youth and surefootedness, she hadn't been very clever up there on Starry Rock, had she? Averil reached out and caught her sister's hand. 'I'm sorry, Sal. It must have been bad.'

Eliot, one arm resting on the mantelpiece, said, 'I'd

been out all day, as luck would have it. There was a note in the post this morning from that friend of mine near Padstow—the one I looked up the other day. He invited me to go over, so I left the cottage about eleven this morning, and didn't know what was going on until I got back about half an hour ago. I saw Sara in the village and found out what had happened. She was going round enquiring if anyone had seen you.'

Averil said curiously, 'Eliot, why did you leave your windcheater on the top of Starry Rock?'

'So that's why you went over there, was it?'

She nodded. 'Yes, I saw the blob of colour and I thought you were over there. I wanted to tell you I was leaving, and to say goodbye. And then when I got there your friend the yellow-legs was doing his stuff, and I sat for ages not daring to move. Like you taught me years ago,' she added.

Sara said, 'There you are, Eliot, it's all your fault.' But her eyes were warm and soft as she looked at him.

'Too true it is.' He looked repentantly at Averil. 'I'm really sorry. As a matter of interest, I left my coat up there as a sort of experiment. I reckoned that if I could get the yellow-legs accustomed to seeing it around, then perhaps he wouldn't take exception to me if I were inside. Stupid, really!'

Sara moved restlessly. 'Eliot, I think we ought to be getting in touch with Doctor French. That's a nasty deep cut on Averil's leg and I'm sure he'll think she should have some sort of protection. Penicillin, or something.'

'Yes, you're right. Sorry I haven't a phone here. We could go back to the Cormorant and ring him from there. Or better still, we could drive over to his place and fetch him. Shall we go?'

Sara looked at Averil. 'Do you mind if we leave

you for a while? Will you be all right?'

Bill hadn't spoken all this time. Now he moved forward out of the shadow and stood behind Averil's chair, putting a hand on her shoulder. 'She'll be all right,' he said.

Something in his voice made Sara look quickly from his face to her sister's, and back again. What she saw there made her smile softly as she joined Eliot at the door.

When they had gone the little room seemed very quiet, with only the crackle of the logs on the fire. Bill came round and settled himself on the rug at Averil's feet and covered her bandaged hands gently with his. 'I must be very careful with you just now,' he said. 'But just you wait until those bandages are off.'

It was really happening, it wasn't a dream, but still she could hardly believe he was here. She said, 'Why did you come back so soon? I didn't think you—I didn't expect to see you again.'

He laughed, a deep sound that echoed round the cottage room. 'You don't know me very well, do you?'

'I don't think I know you at all,' she said in a very small voice, and he laughed again.

'Why worry? I'm not all that deep, you know. Just an ordinary sort of bloke. I intended to come back as soon as I'd settled up a couple of important matters with the Old Bird in town. You see, I couldn't bring myself to tell you, but he bought the Cormorant to live in when he retires, which will be quite soon.'

'I know,' she said. 'Louella told me.'

His head jerked up. 'The devil she did! I told her particularly that the whole thing was to be kept quiet, until I'd seen that Sara would be fixed up in something else. What the blazes did she want to tell you for?'

It was the first time she had seen him angry and it

was quite an experience.

'I don't suppose she realised what it meant to us—to Sara and me,' she said. But she *had* realised. She wasn't the girl to say anything without calculating the effect. She had wanted to score off Averil, for some reason, and she had succeeded. 'It doesn't matter now,' she said.

'No, as it happens it doesn't,' Bill agreed, but he still sounded annoyed, 'but Louella wasn't to know that. That was one of the things I had to go into with the Old Bird. I'd forgotten his genius for organisation. He had several alternative offers for Sara, as it happens. But I don't think she'll be taking up any of them, do you?'

'You mean—Sara and Eliot?'

'Precisely,' he said.

She sat up. 'Has he told you?'

'Well,' said Bill judicially, 'he hasn't spelled it out, but I have eyes in my head. And so have you, my sweet.'

'I couldn't let myself believe it. It's been so long and she was so hurt, and when Eliot came back she was so stiff and prickly with him.' She sighed with delight. 'Well, isn't that wonderful!'

'I think so,' said Bill quietly.

She laid her head against the back of the chair. He was so close; she only had to move her hand a few inches to touch his hair. But she did not dare, for still she didn't know where she, Averil, came into all this, or even if she came into it at all.

She said, 'What was the other important thing?'

He clasped his hands round his knees and stared into the fire. 'Have you ever had to hurt someone you cared about?' he said. 'I had to tell the Old Bird that I was going to let him down—that I couldn't see myself in the hotel business at all. I came down here determined to give it a try, to get interested in it, and at first, at the Cormorant, I thought I might. I liked the place and the atmosphere and the way your sister coped with things. But then when Louella showed me the real Raven set-up, at the Cliff, I just knew it wasn't for me and never would be, and the only honest thing was to break the news to my grandfather. I only hoped he wouldn't be too hurt and disappointed.'

' And was he?'

Suddenly Bill chuckled. ' He's a great guy, the Old Bird, you'll like him. He didn't turn a hair. He said, " Don't worry, my boy. I've had about enough of the hotel business myself. I had an excellent offer for Raven Hotels last week and you've cleared my way to accepting it." When I told him that Eliot Dunn had invited me to link up with his crew and start a bigger and better team he got very enthusiastic. He has offered to back us up to the hilt, believe it or not. He had it all planned out in ten minutes flat, which is typical of the Old Bird. He's going to move to the Cormorant in the autumn and make it the head-quarters of the team. That way he'll be kept abreast of what's going on. What do you think of that?'

She said, ' You've—you've taken my breath away.' She felt very cold. All this had nothing to do with her. She wasn't connected with the 'two important matters' he had to settle. He hadn't come back to see her; in any case, he couldn't have expected that she would still be here, for she had told him that she was going back to Exeter last Friday. A dull misery began to settle inside her. When she looked at it squarely, nothing that Bill had said or done since he had taken her off the Rock had changed anything between them. His manner to her was just the same as it had always been

—lighthearted, half teasing.

She sat there numb and silent, wishing he had never come back. How could she hope to get him out of her mind and her heart if he were going into partnership with Eliot? It just made everything worse than ever.

Abruptly he swung round and the lamplight was full on his face. 'It all depends on you, you know.'

He wasn't teasing now. What she saw in his eyes made her pulses leap wildly. 'On m-me? But why?'

He drew in a breath. 'Because everything I do from now on depends on you. Because if you're not with me it doesn't really matter *what* I do. Because that's the way I love you. You believe me?'

She said slowly, wonderingly, 'I believe you, because that's the way I love you, too.'

In the lamplight and the firelight their eyes met and held. Then Averil whispered, 'What's a few scratches, anyway?' and she slid to the hearthrug beside him and turned into his arms.

Much later she said, her face in the hollow of his neck, 'I thought you'd gone away for good. Why didn't you tell me?'

'I was scared.'

She giggled. Bill scared? 'You don't expect me to believe that?'

'It's the truth, cross my heart. I found I was getting serious about a girl for the first time in my life, and I didn't know how to handle it. And you weren't any sort of girl, you were a girl with a mind of her own, a career of her own, heading for success. Also, your sister looked on me as the enemy, and with a certain amount of reason. And to cap it all, I wasn't quite sure whether the Old Bird would cut me off with a new penny when I said my piece. So I couldn't tell you, not until I knew what I had to offer you.' His

191

arm tightened round her. 'I think I was born lucky, because it's all worked out.' He kissed her again and again and each time it was a new delight.

Presently she said, 'Did you tell your grandfather about me?'

'Of course I did. I warned him that I hadn't asked you, that I wasn't sure if you'd have me, but he wouldn't hear a word of that. If you'd turned me down you'd have had him to reckon with, and he's a demon for getting his own way. Already he's planning how best to divide the Cormorant up into two houses —one for him and one for us. And you are to have the annexe fitted up as a studio—would you like that?'

'Love it,' she said dreamily. 'But the annexe is much too big for a studio.'

'The other part might be turned into a nursery,' suggested Bill nonchalantly, 'for use when you get tired of roaming the world with me. You see, the Old Bird isn't the only one in the family who can make plans. Anyway, the Obby Oss picked you out to carry on the human race, and he was a magic Oss.'

She said, smiling to herself, 'I couldn't possibly let him down.'

She began to sing the tune of the May Song, softly, and after a while he joined in. When the others came back they were still singing, their arms close about each other, two people lost in the oldest magic in the world.